JOKER

by Anthony Masters

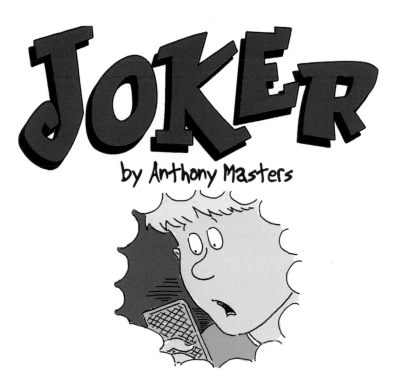

ILLUSTRATED BY MICHAEL REID
COLORS BY JEANA LIDFORS

Librarian Reviewer
Laurie K. Holland
Media Specialist (National Board Certified), Edina, MN
MA in Elementary Education, Minnesota State University, Mankato, MN

Reading Consultant
Sherry Klehr
Elementary/Middle School Educator, Edina Public Schools, MN
MA in Education, University of Minnesota, MN

 **STONE ARCH BOOKS**
Minneapolis   San Diego

First published in the United States in 2006
by Stone Arch Books,
151 Good Counsel Drive, P.O. Box 669,
Mankato, Minnesota 56002.
www.stonearchbooks.com

Originally published in Great Britain in 2000
by A & C Black Publishers Ltd.

Library of Congress Cataloging-in-Publication Data
Masters, Anthony.
    Joker / by Anthony Masters; illustrated by Michael Reid.
    p. cm. — (Graphic Trax)
    ISBN-13: 978-1-59889-024-2 (hardcover)
    ISBN-10: 1-59889-024-7 (hardcover)
    1. Graphic novels. I. Reid, Michael, Illustrator. II. Title. III. Series.
PN6727.M246J66 2006
741.5—dc22   2005026692

Summary: Mel loves magic tricks and practical jokes. But when his dad, Magic Max, is
kidnapped, no one believes him. Everyone thinks Mel is joking.

1 2 3 4 5 6 11 10 09 08 07 06

Printed in the United States of America.

TABLE OF CONTENTS

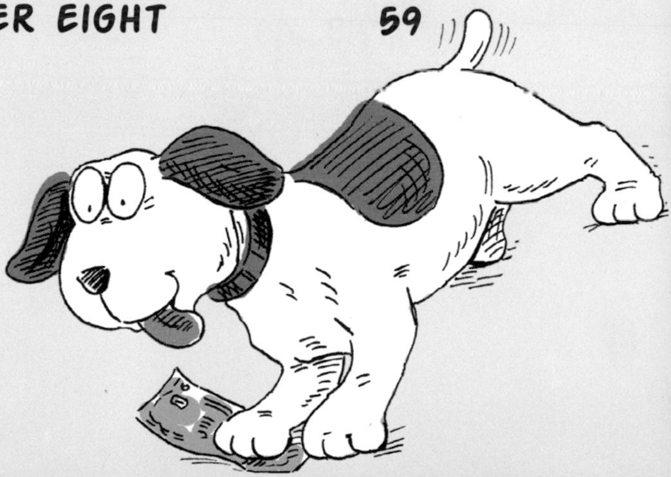

**MUTT
(MEL'S DOG)**

**MAGIC MAX
(MEL'S DAD)**

MEL

PAUL

TIM

CHAPTER ONE

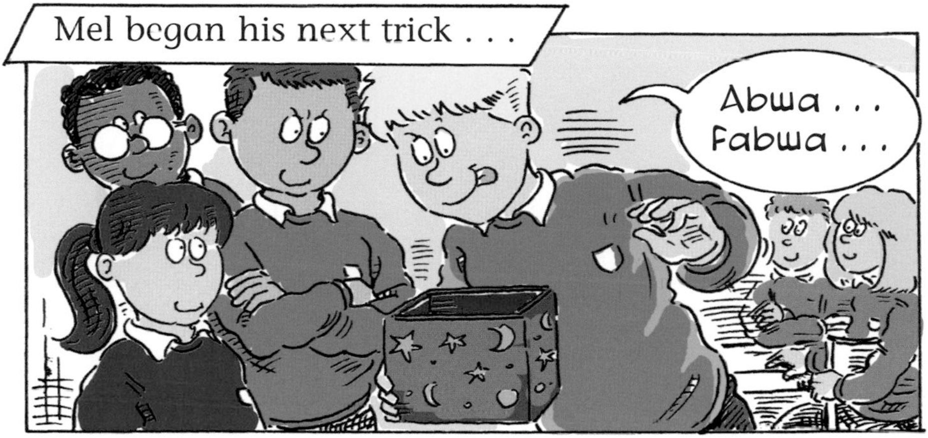
Mel began his next trick . . .
Abwa . . . Fabwa . . .

Mel had never messed up a trick before, but there was always a first time. And this trick wasn't easy.

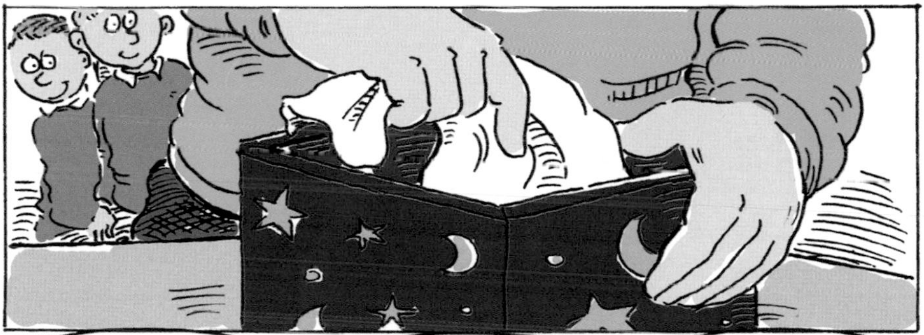

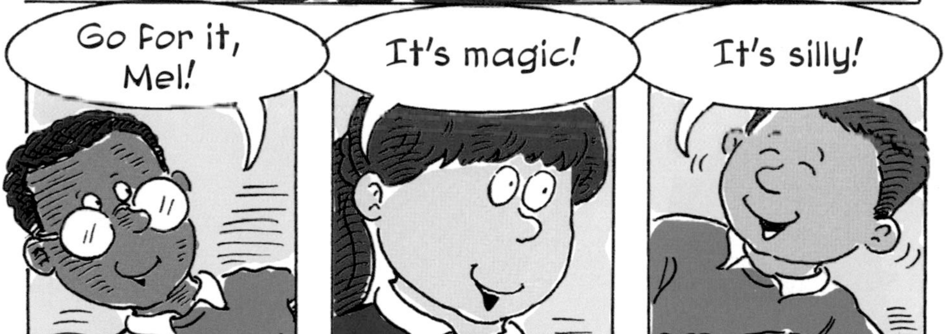
Go for it, Mel!
It's magic!
It's silly!

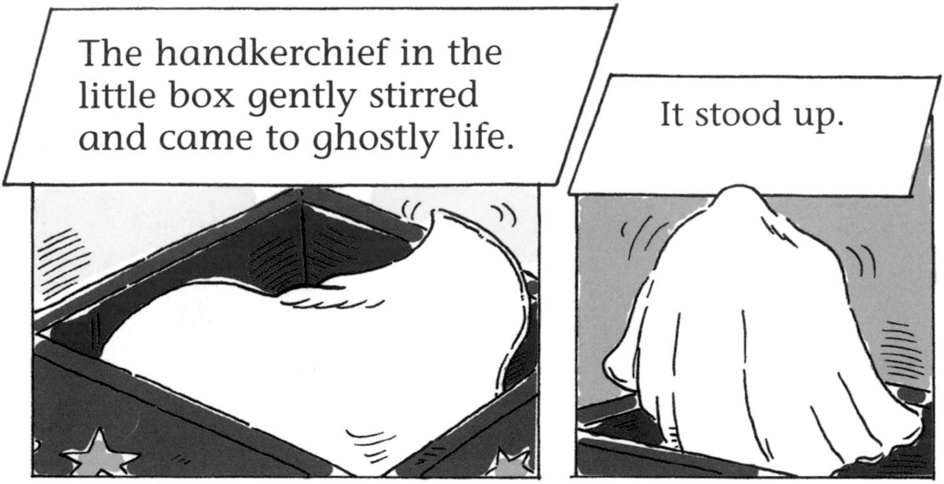
The handkerchief in the little box gently stirred and came to ghostly life.
It stood up.

Slowly, the handkerchief began to follow Mel around the classroom. Then it jumped into his hand as if it were alive.

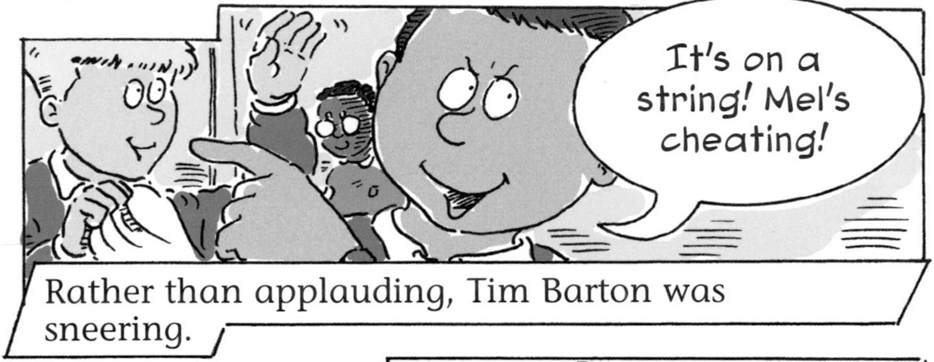
It's on a string! Mel's cheating!
Rather than applauding, Tim Barton was sneering.

Tim grabbed the string and pulled the handkerchief along the floor. The scornful laughter went on for a long time. Even Mel's best friend, Paul, was grinning.

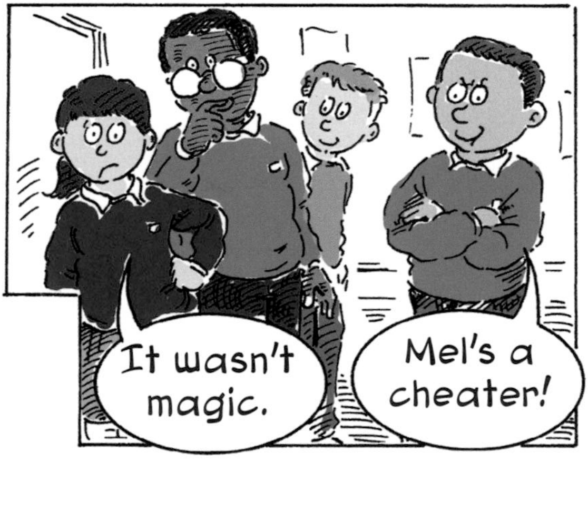
It wasn't magic.
Mel's a cheater!

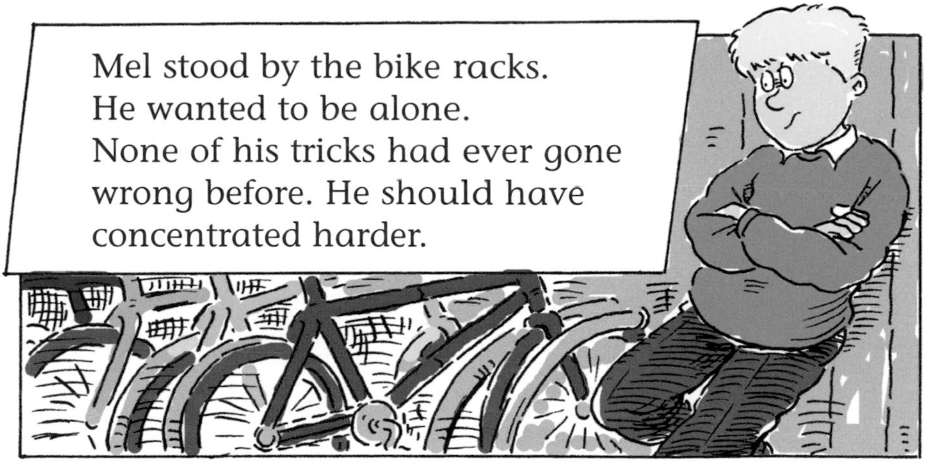
Mel stood by the bike racks.
He wanted to be alone.
None of his tricks had ever gone
wrong before. He should have
concentrated harder.

Mel was frustrated.

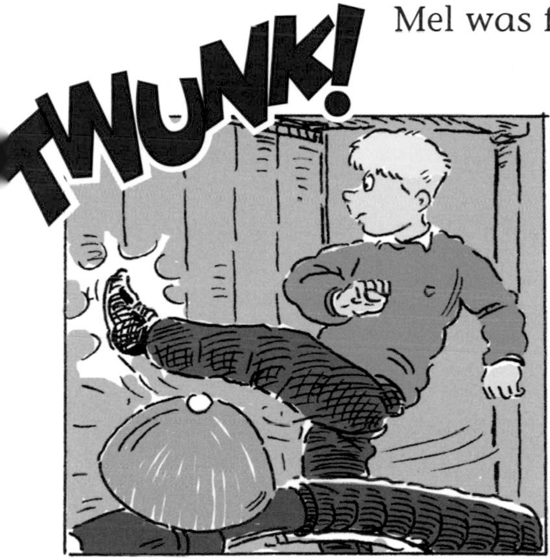
TWUNK!

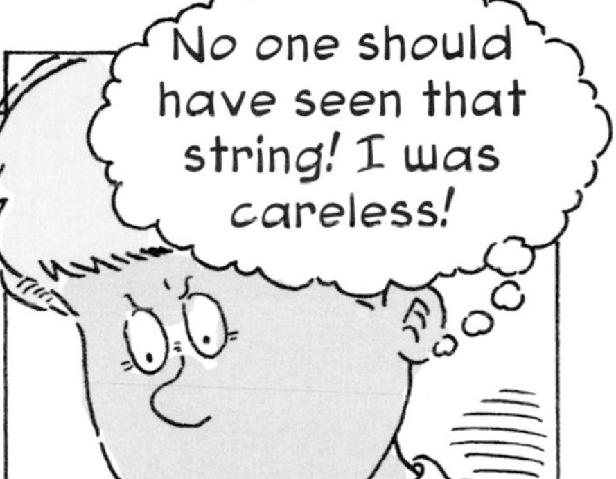
No one should have seen that string! I was careless!

Mel thought of his dog, Mutt. Dad brought him home after Mom left. Mutt was his best friend now. Not Paul. Not anyone. Just Mutt.

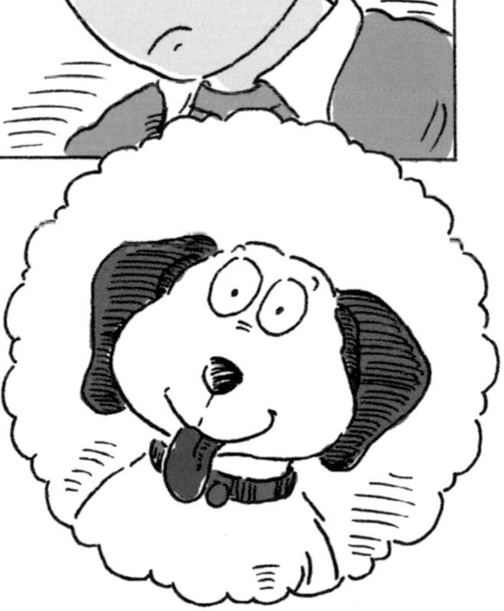

Meanwhile, on the playground . . .

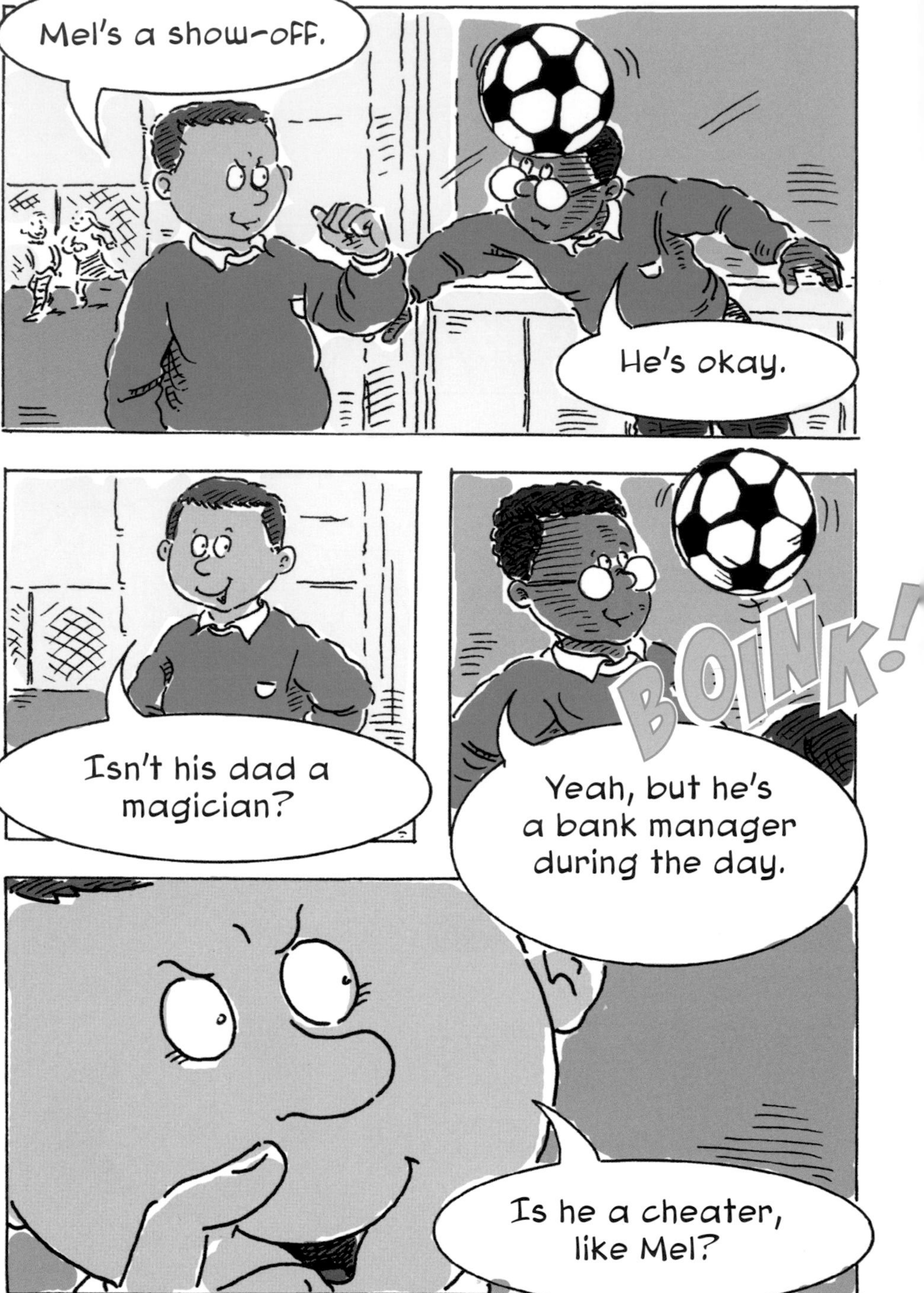
Mel's a show-off.
He's okay.
Isn't his dad a magician?
BOINK!
Yeah, but he's a bank manager during the day.
Is he a cheater, like Mel?

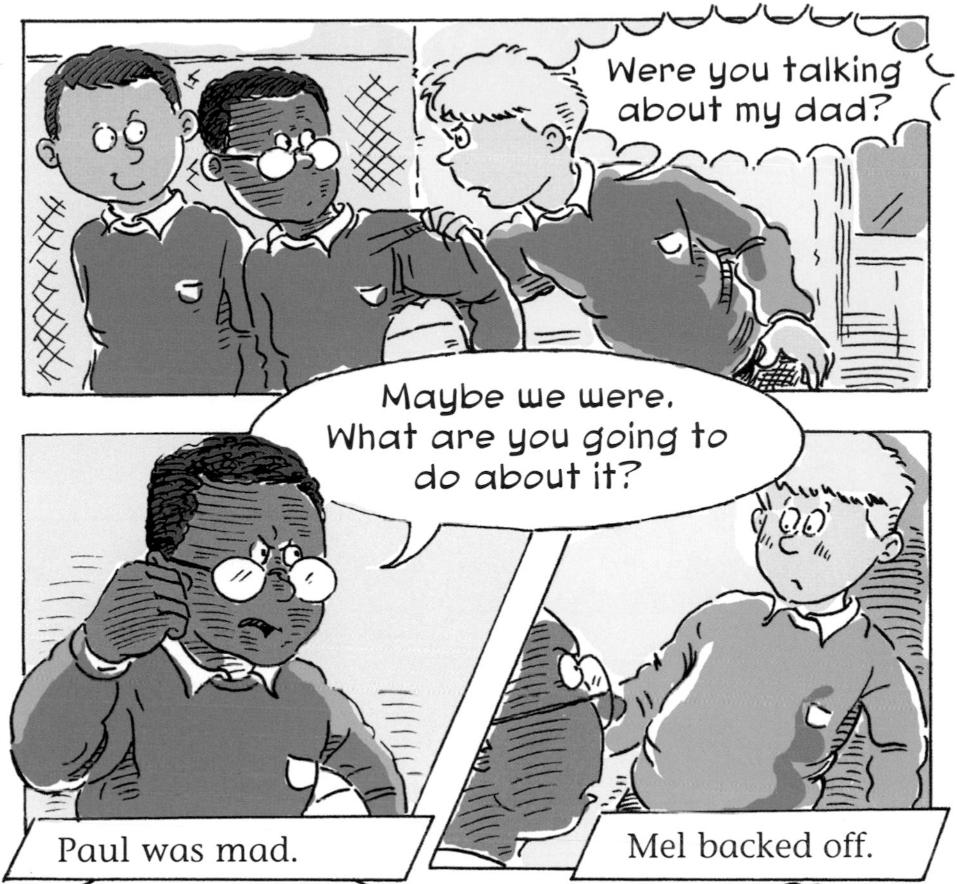
Were you talking about my dad?
Maybe we were. What are you going to do about it?
Paul was mad.
Mel backed off.

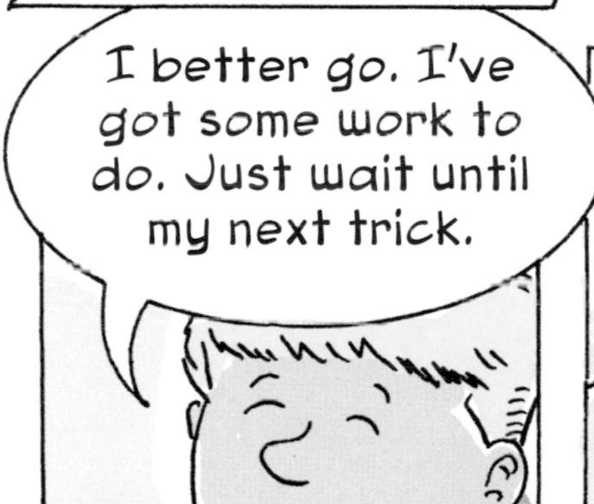
I better go. I've got some work to do. Just wait until my next trick.

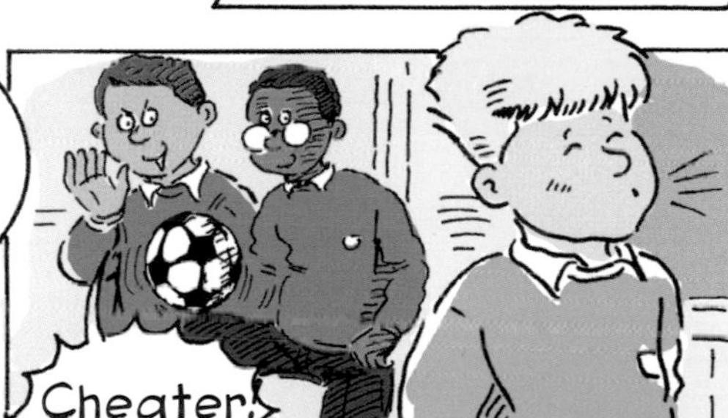
Cheater!

Mel walked away, whistling. Paul knew his friend was trying to show off again.

CHAPTER TWO

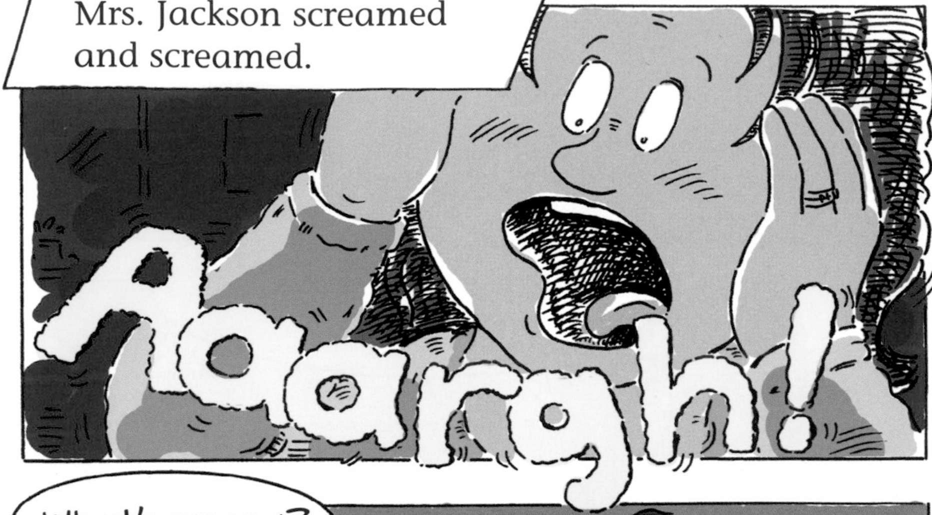
Mrs. Jackson screamed and screamed.
Aaargh!

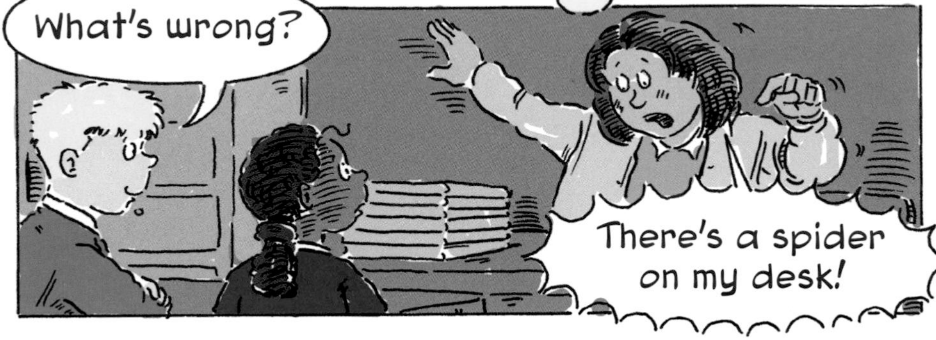
What's wrong?
There's a spider on my desk!

The class crowded around her. There was a huge hairy spider sitting there.

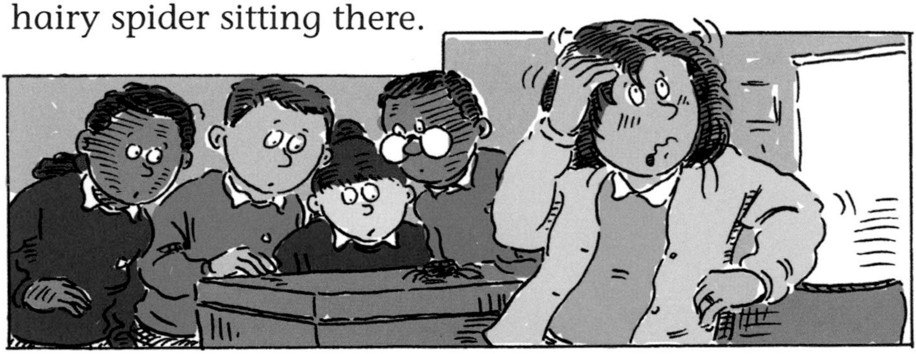

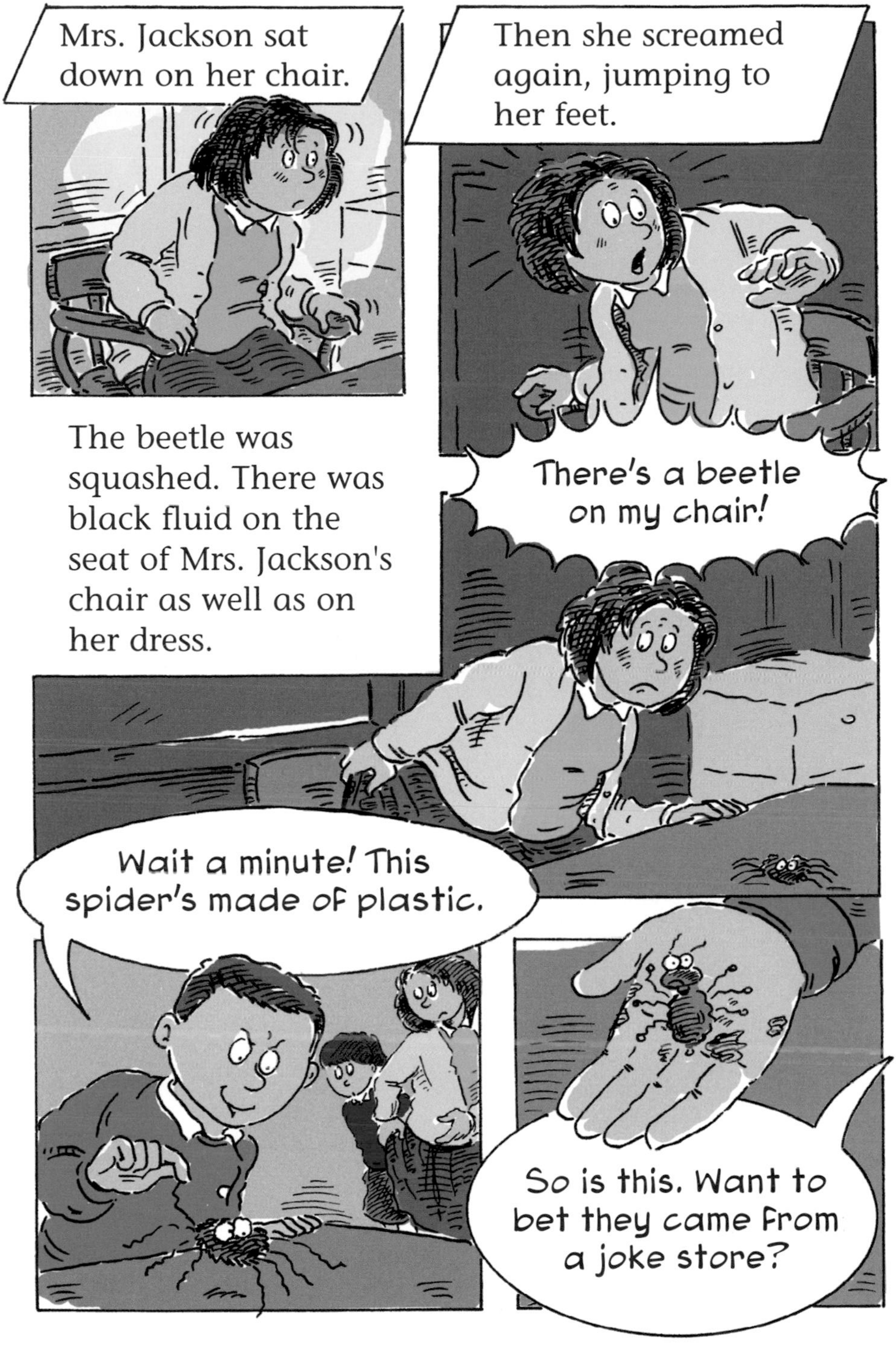
Mrs. Jackson sat down on her chair.
Then she screamed again, jumping to her feet.
There's a beetle on my chair!
The beetle was squashed. There was black fluid on the seat of Mrs. Jackson's chair as well as on her dress.
Wait a minute! This spider's made of plastic.
So is this. Want to bet they came from a joke store?

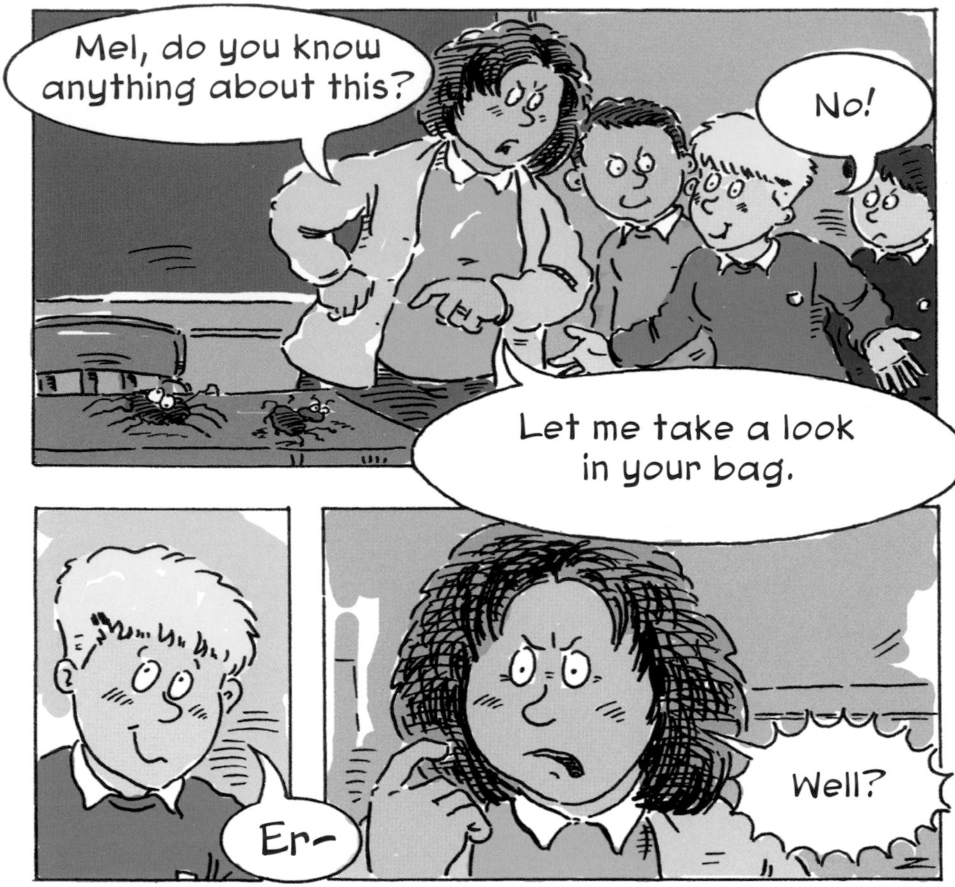
Mel, do you know anything about this?
No!
Let me take a look in your bag.
Er–
Well?

For a moment, Mel was frozen to the spot.

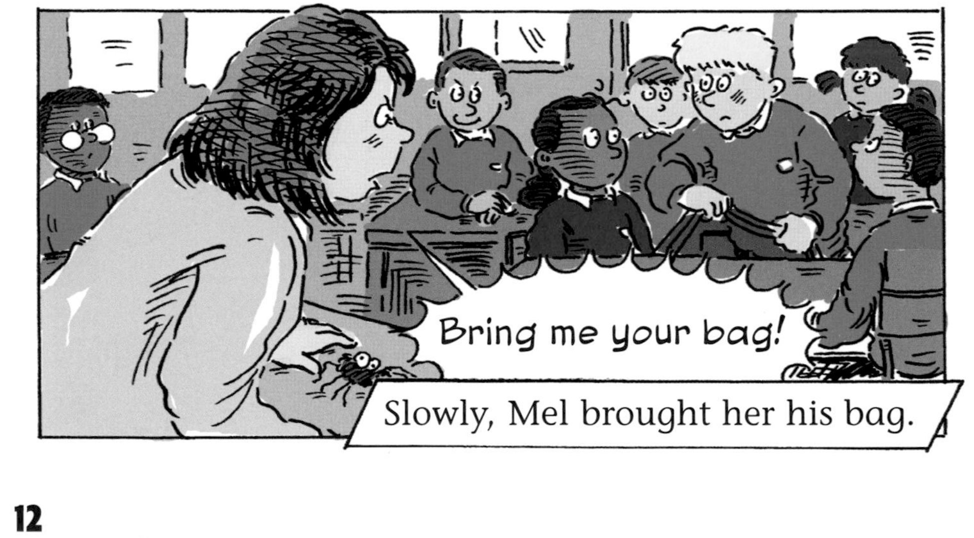
Bring me your bag!
Slowly, Mel brought her his bag.

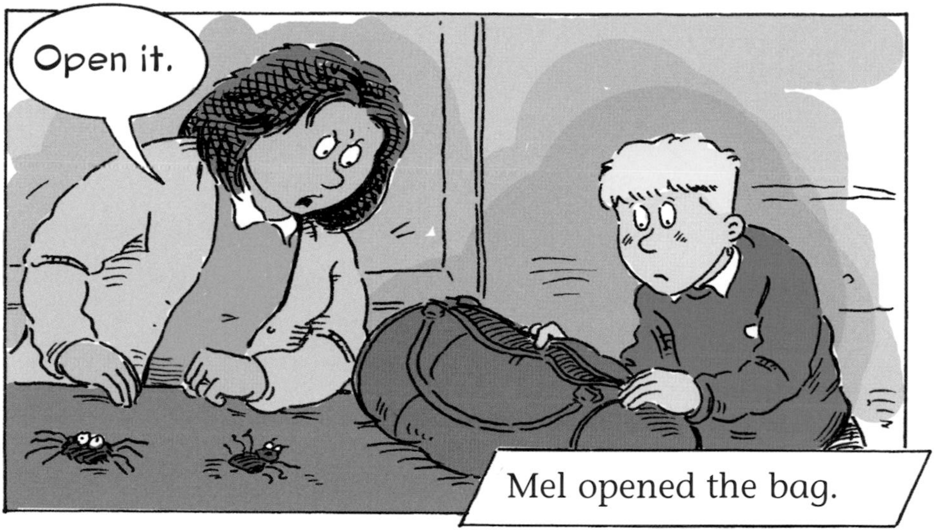
Open it.
Mel opened the bag.

Mrs. Jackson plunged her hand inside the bag and pulled out another plastic spider and a couple of stink bombs as well.

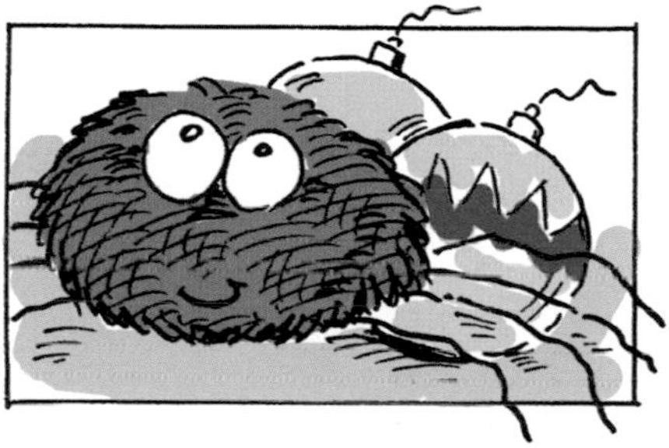

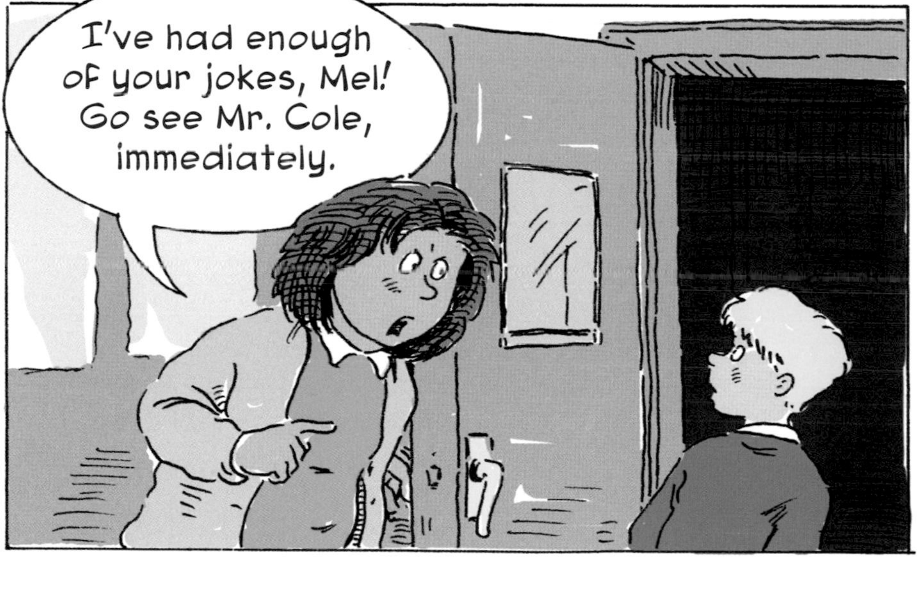
I've had enough of your jokes, Mel! Go see Mr. Cole, immediately.

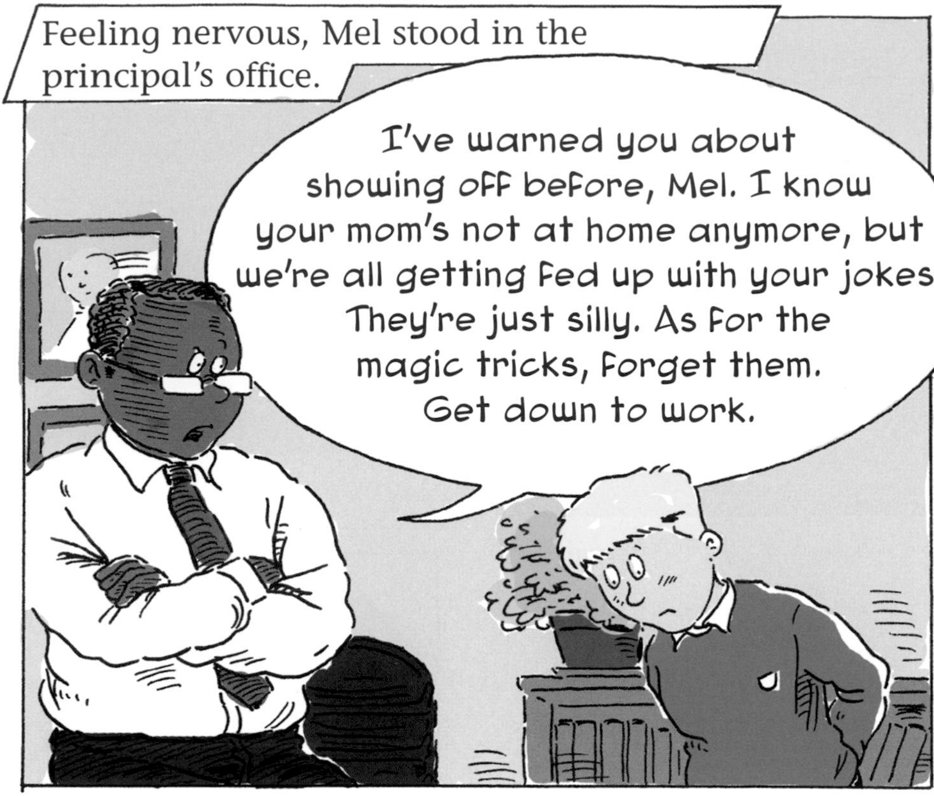
Feeling nervous, Mel stood in the principal's office.
I've warned you about showing off before, Mel. I know your mom's not at home anymore, but we're all getting fed up with your jokes. They're just silly. As for the magic tricks, forget them. Get down to work.

Mel was almost in tears.

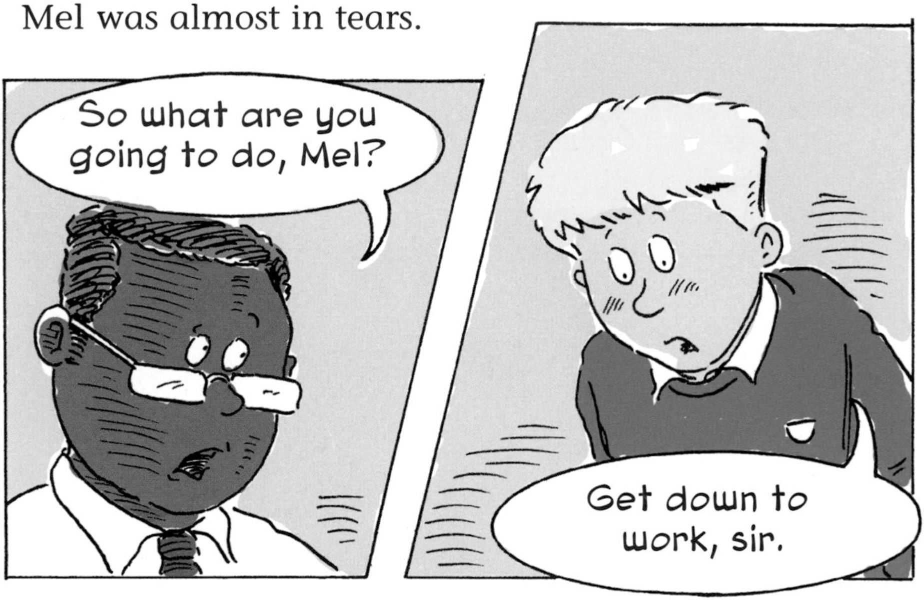
So what are you going to do, Mel?
Get down to work, sir.

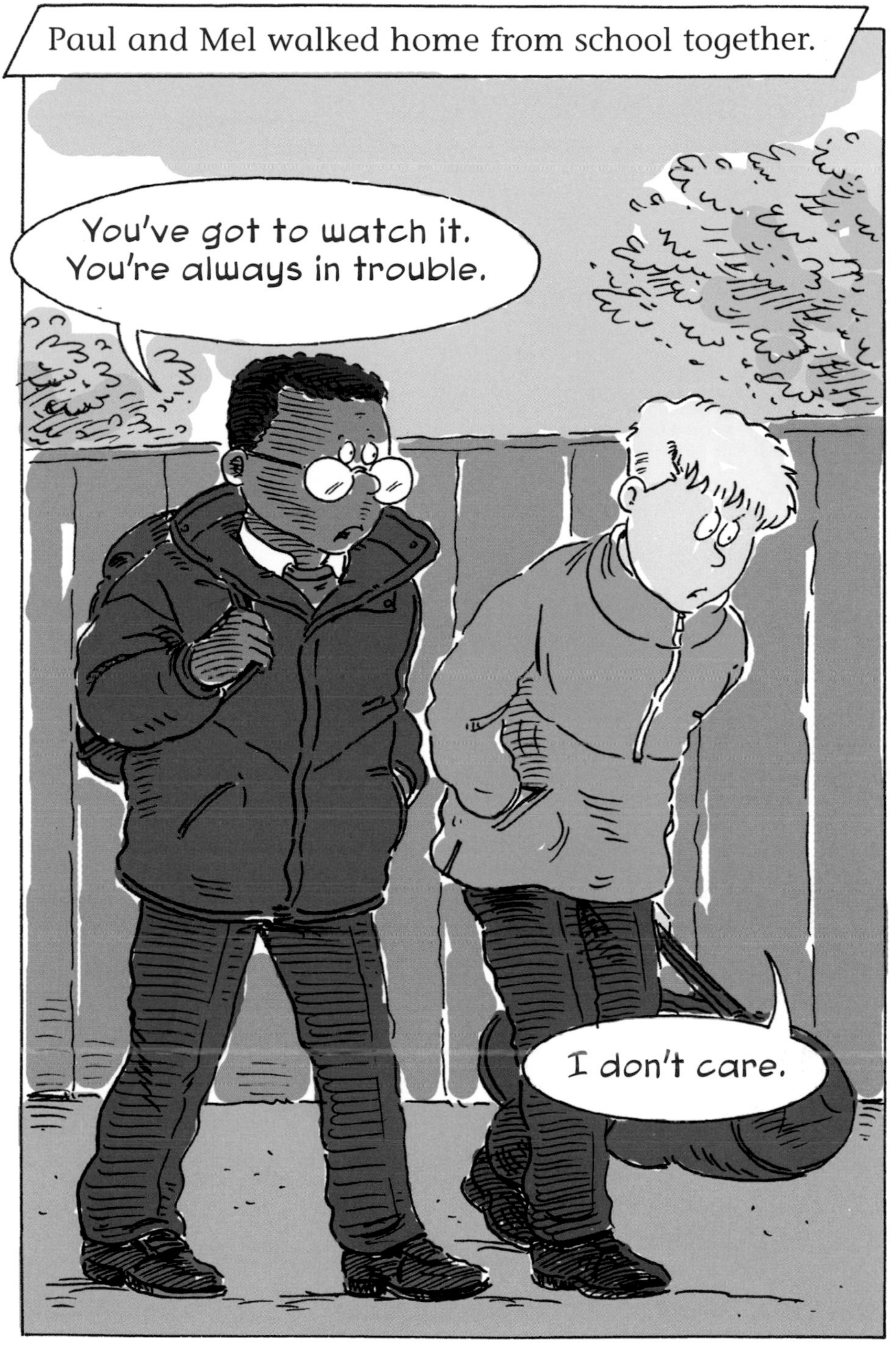
Paul and Mel walked home from school together.
You've got to watch it. You're always in trouble.
I don't care.

Mel could see his father talking to a man outside the front gate of their house. Dad looked worried. Or was that just Mel's imagination?

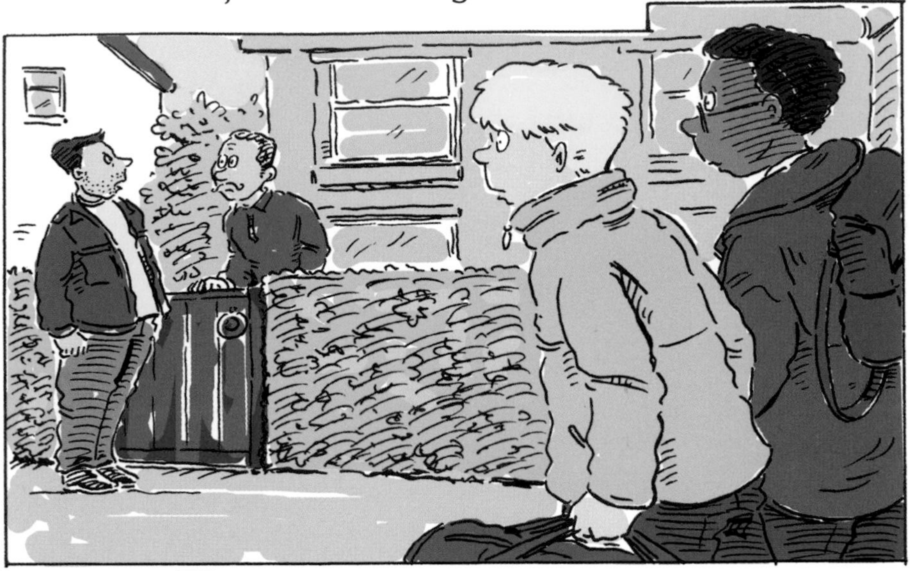

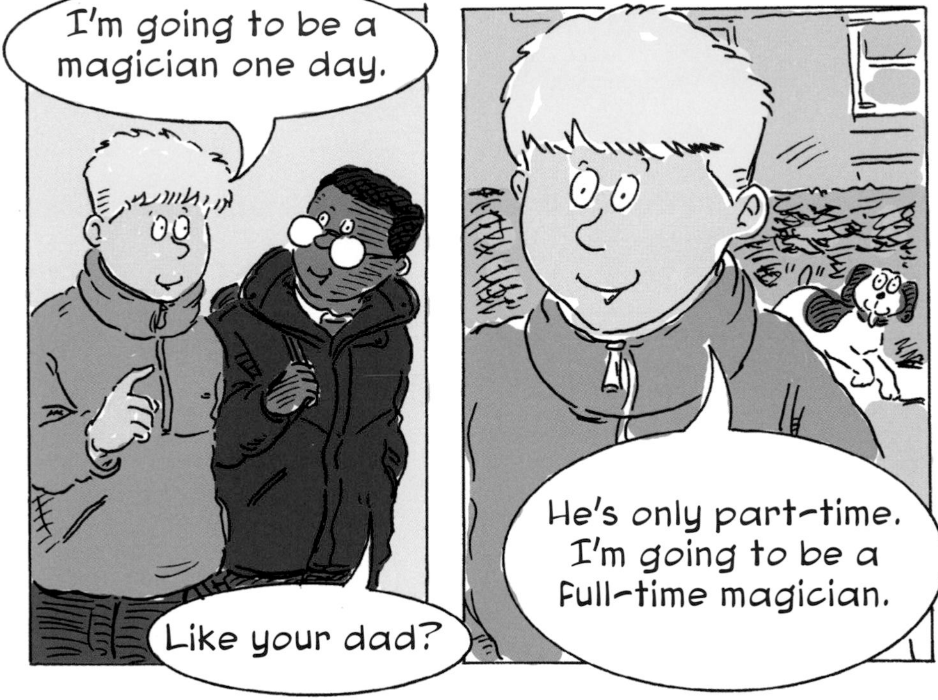
I'm going to be a magician one day.
Like your dad?
He's only part-time. I'm going to be a full-time magician.

Mel was already lost in a daydream. He was on stage, bowing to a huge audience.

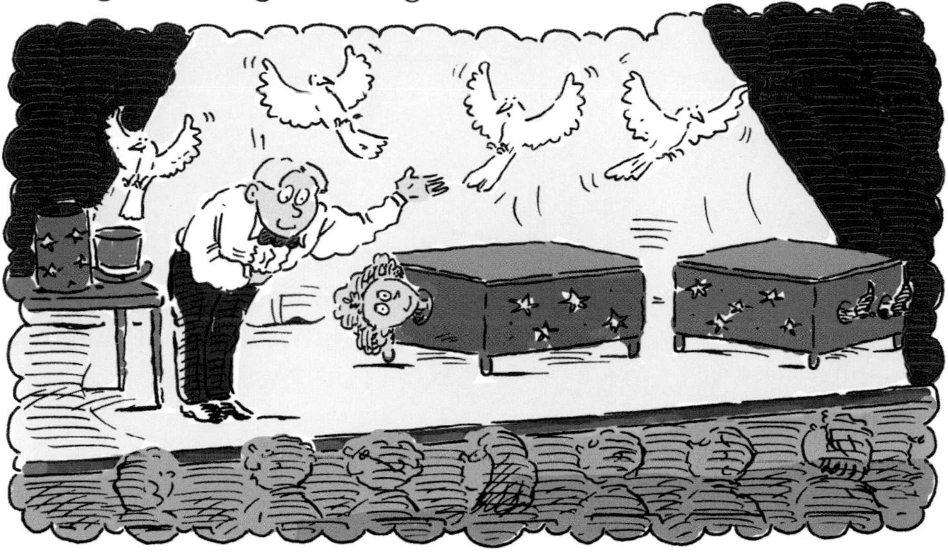

Coming back to reality, Mel saw his best friend, Mutt.

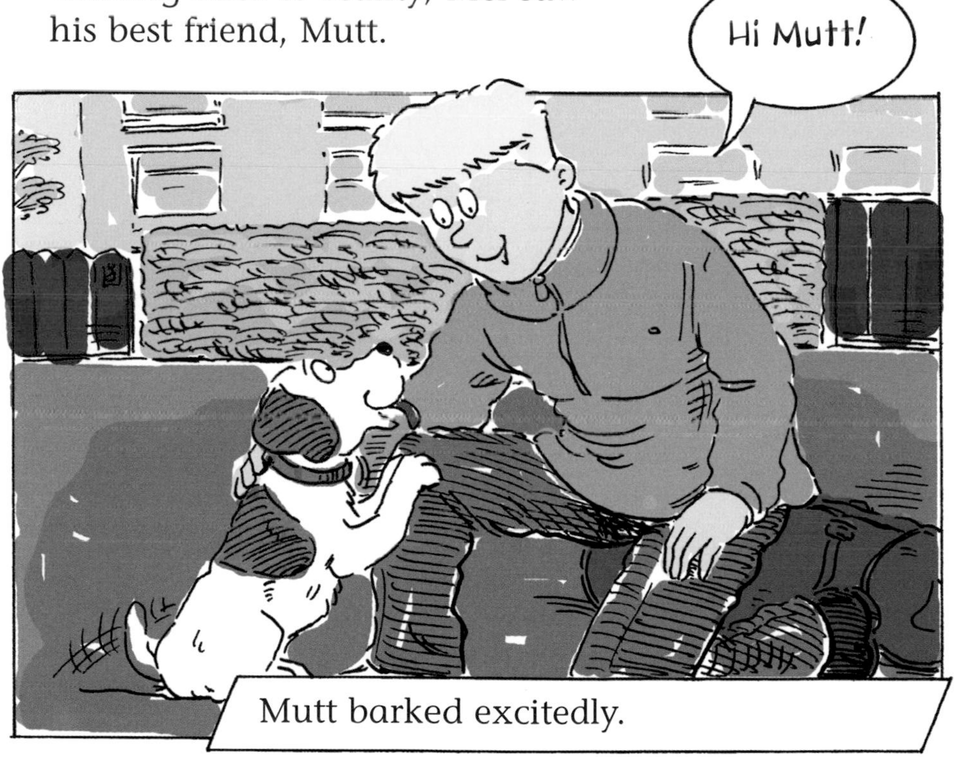
Hi Mutt!
Mutt barked excitedly.

Later that night . . .

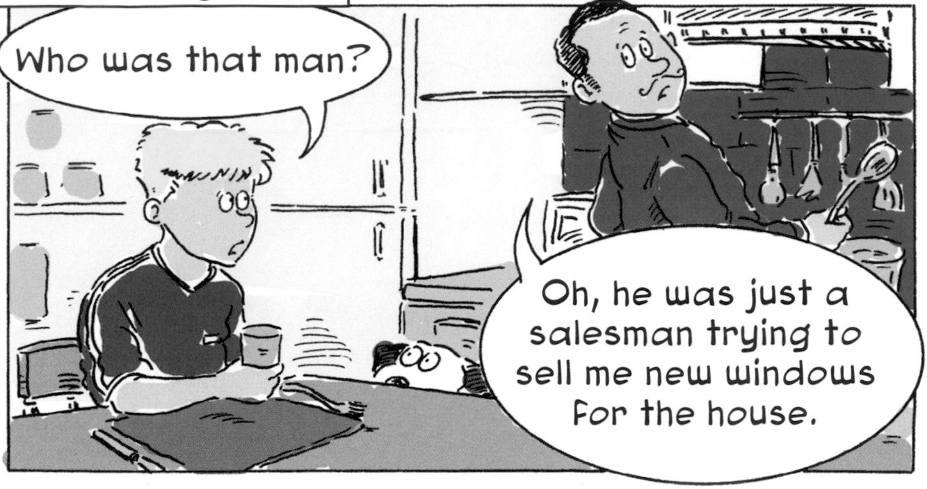

Who was that man?
Oh, he was just a salesman trying to sell me new windows for the house.

Mel gazed at his father suspiciously. He knew his dad was holding something back.

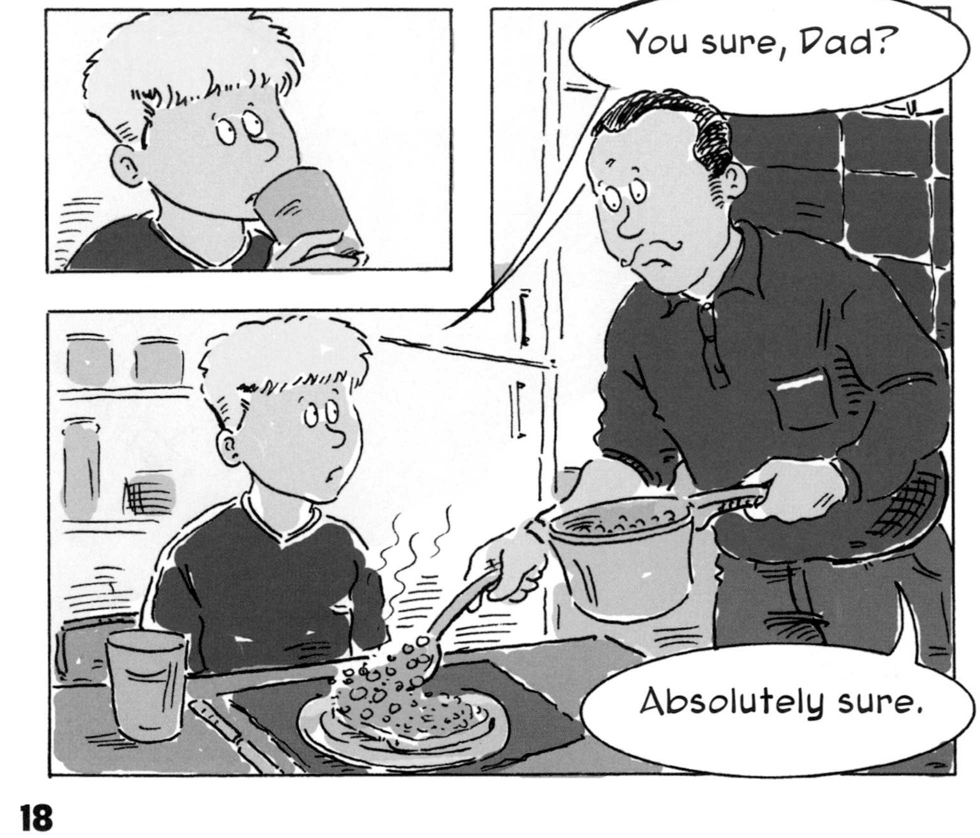

You sure, Dad?
Absolutely sure.

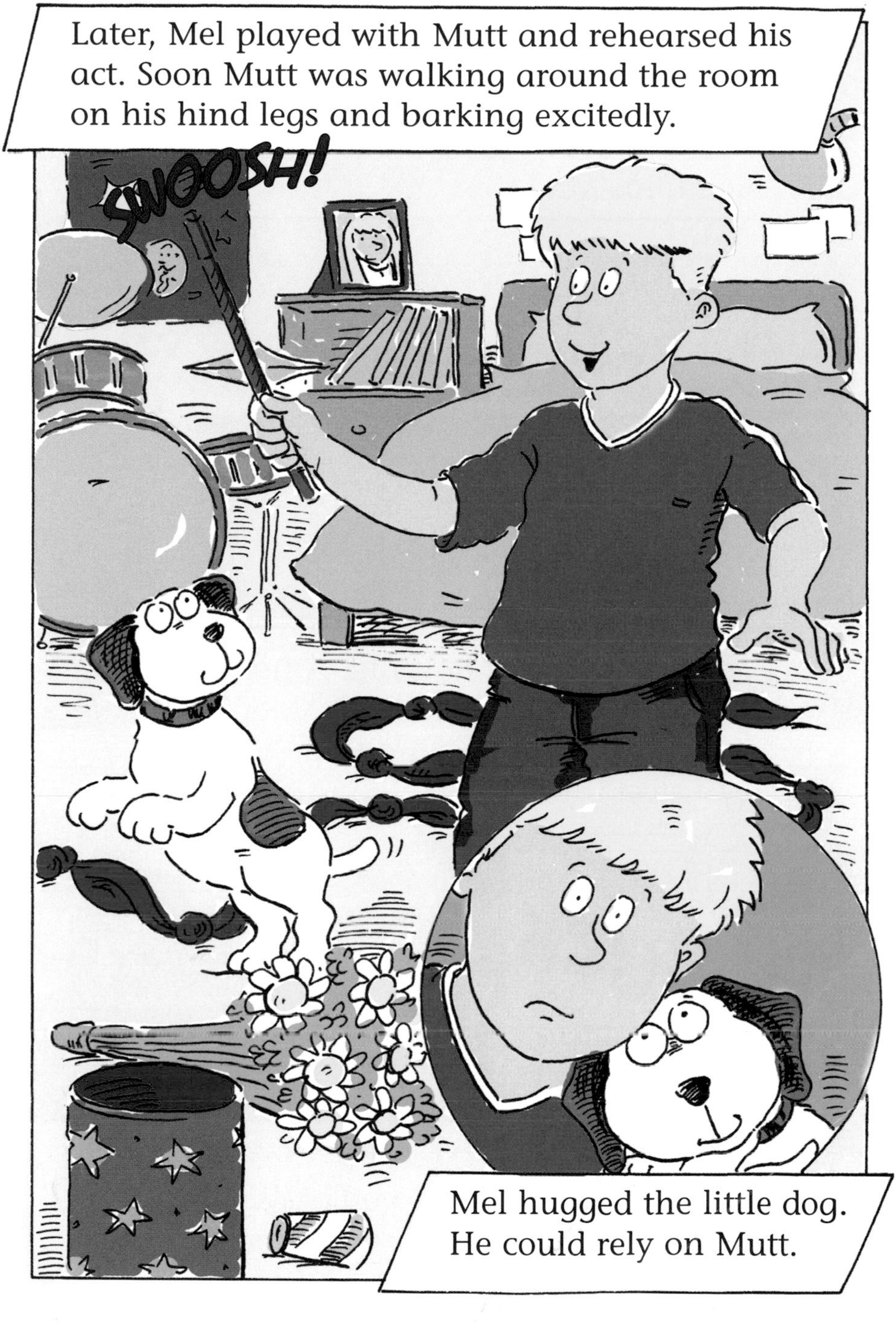
Later, Mel played with Mutt and rehearsed his act. Soon Mutt was walking around the room on his hind legs and barking excitedly.
SWOOSH!
Mel hugged the little dog. He could rely on Mutt.

CHAPTER THREE

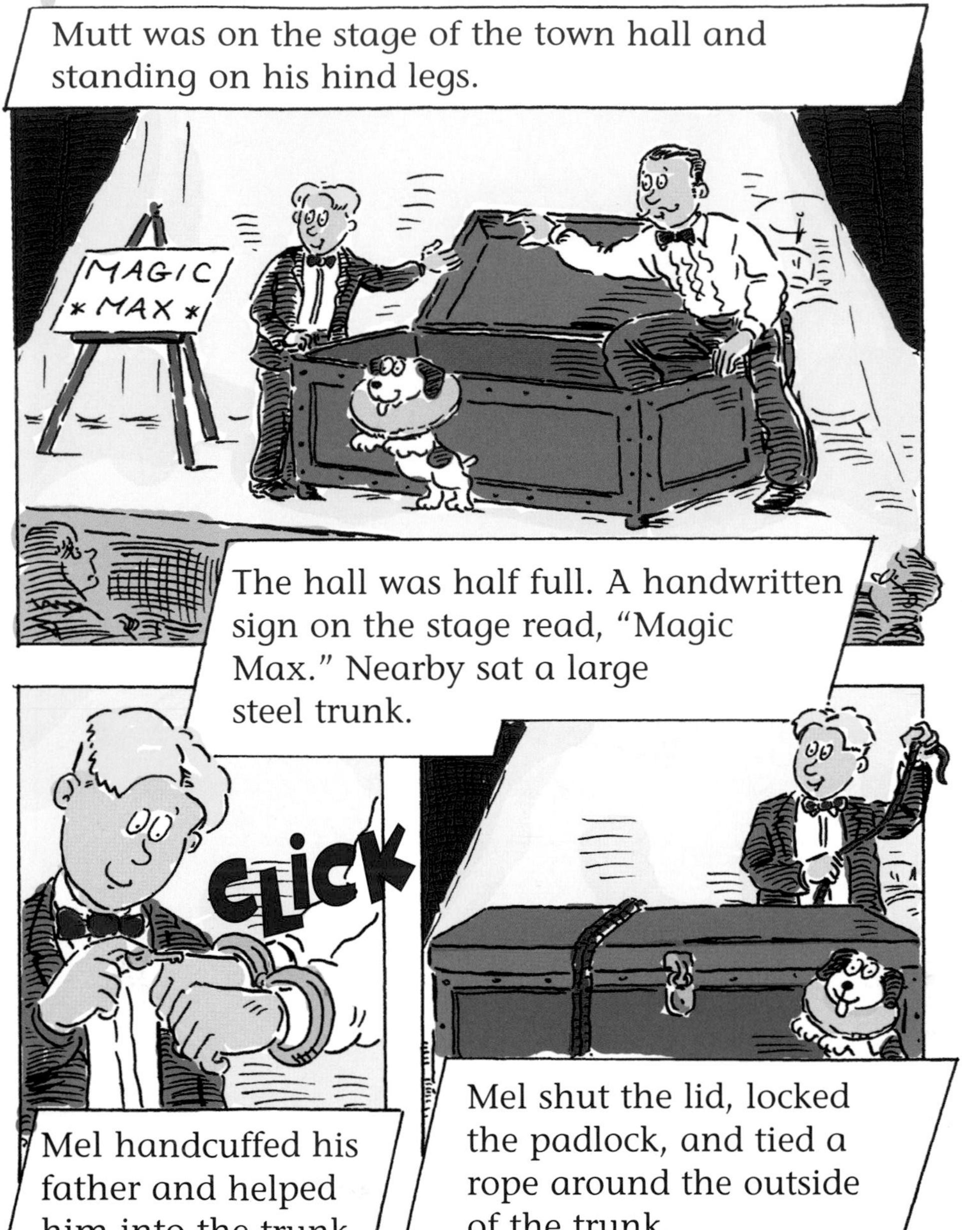
Mutt was on the stage of the town hall and standing on his hind legs.
MAGIC *MAX*
The hall was half full. A handwritten sign on the stage read, "Magic Max." Nearby sat a large steel trunk.
CLICK
Mel handcuffed his father and helped him into the trunk.
Mel shut the lid, locked the padlock, and tied a rope around the outside of the trunk.

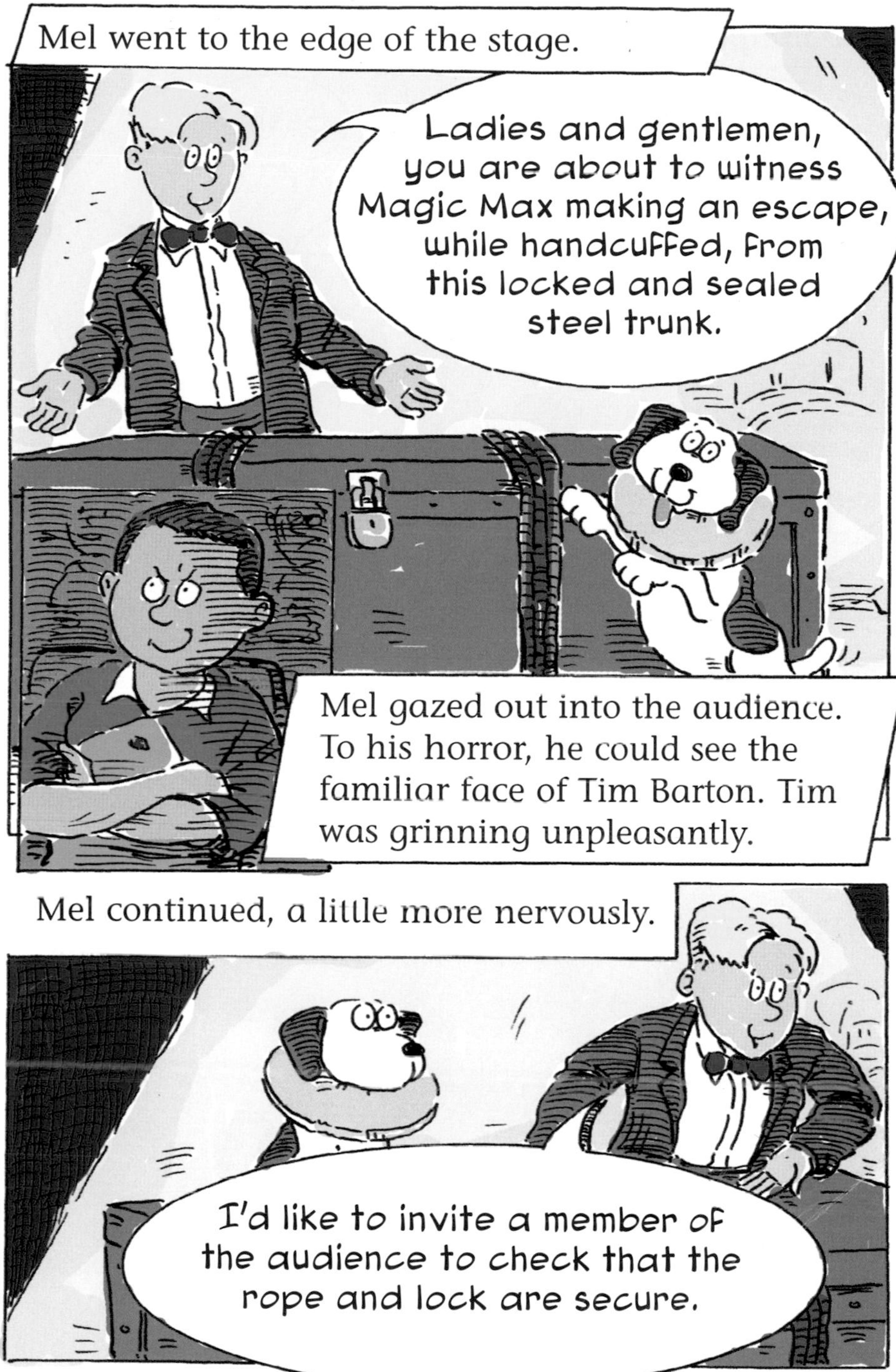
Mel went to the edge of the stage.
Ladies and gentlemen, you are about to witness Magic Max making an escape, while handcuffed, from this locked and sealed steel trunk.
Mel gazed out into the audience. To his horror, he could see the familiar face of Tim Barton. Tim was grinning unpleasantly.
Mel continued, a little more nervously.
I'd like to invite a member of the audience to check that the rope and lock are secure.

Tim jumped to his feet and raced to the stage.

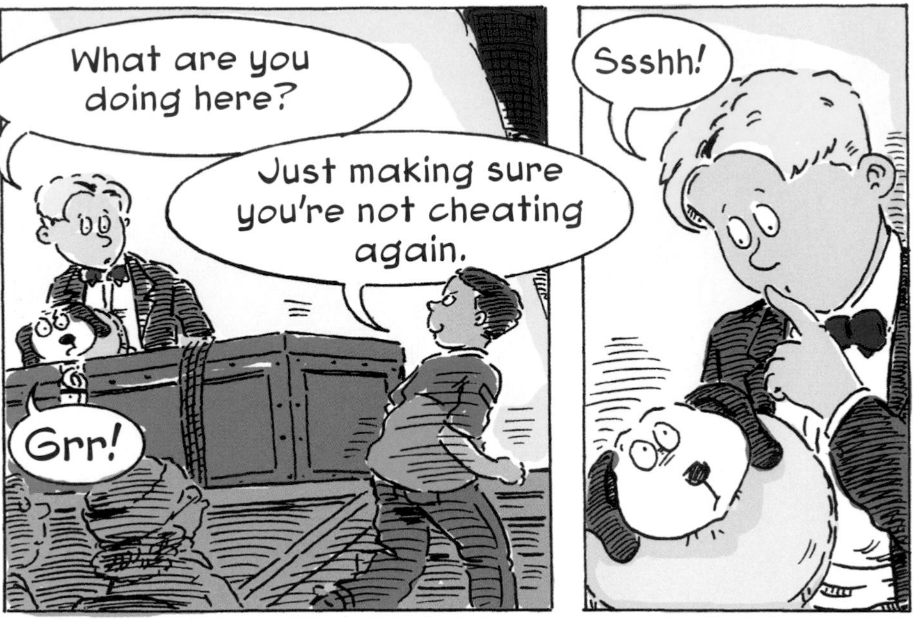
What are you doing here?
Just making sure you're not cheating again.
Grr!
Ssshh!

Tim checked the rope and lock.

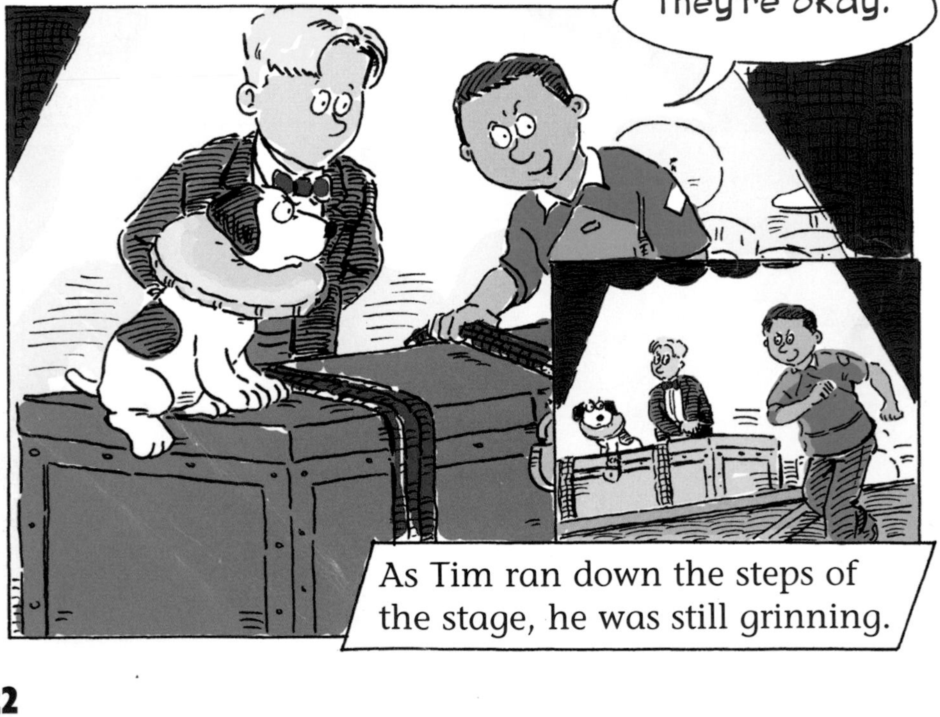
They're okay.
As Tim ran down the steps of the stage, he was still grinning.

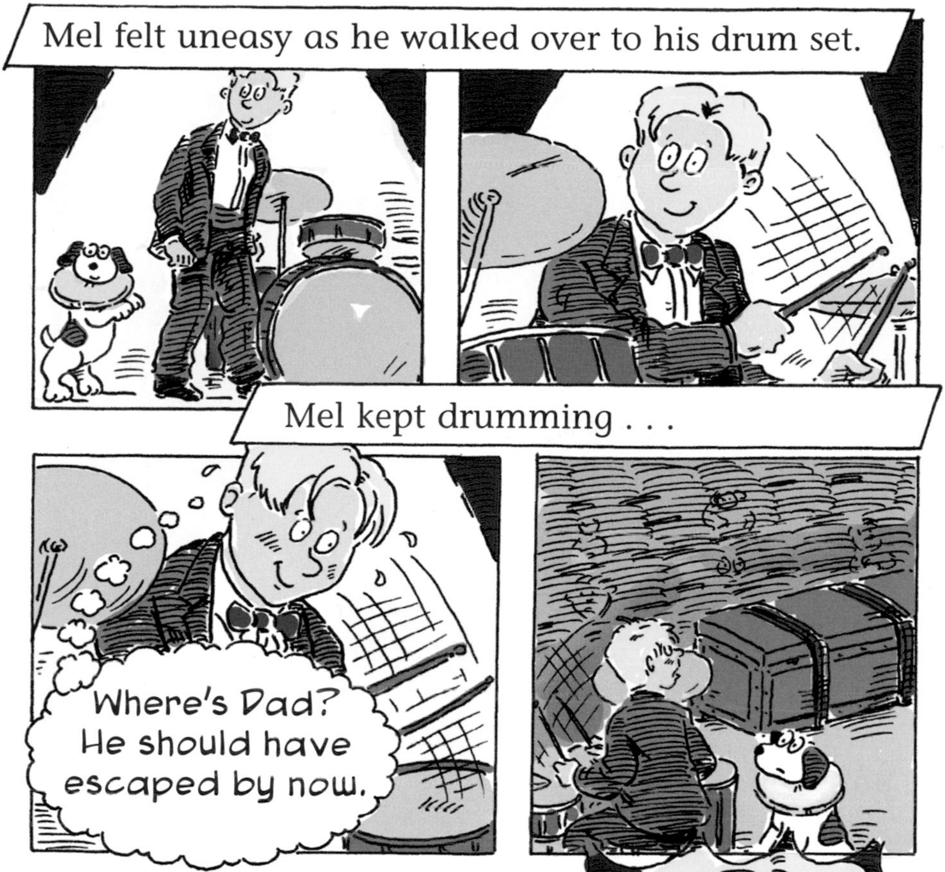
Mel felt uneasy as he walked over to his drum set.
Mel kept drumming . . .
Where's Dad? He should have escaped by now.

Then, from the bottom of the trunk, a joker playing card was pushed out onto the floor of the stage. Mel froze, gasped in horror, and stopped playing the drums.

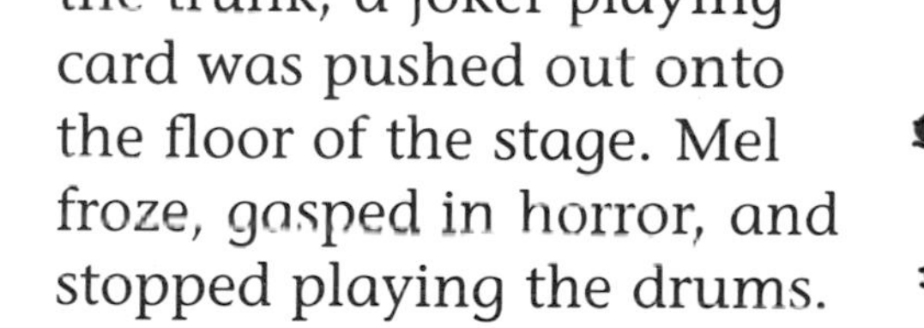

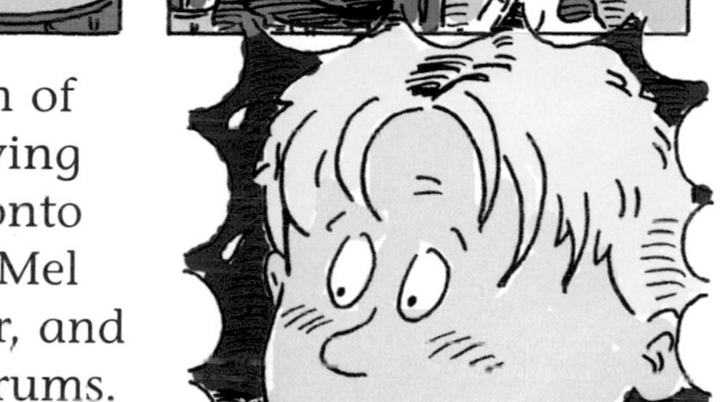
The distress signal!

The joker was the distress signal Mel and his father always had in case something went wrong. Mel hurried off stage and dropped the curtain.

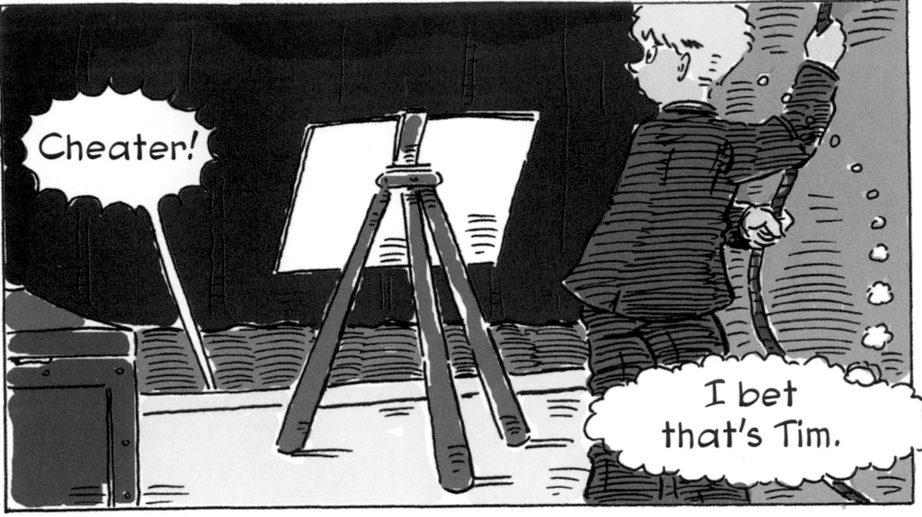
Cheater!
I bet that's Tim.

Once the curtain was lowered, Mel worked quickly, untying the rope and unlocking the lock.

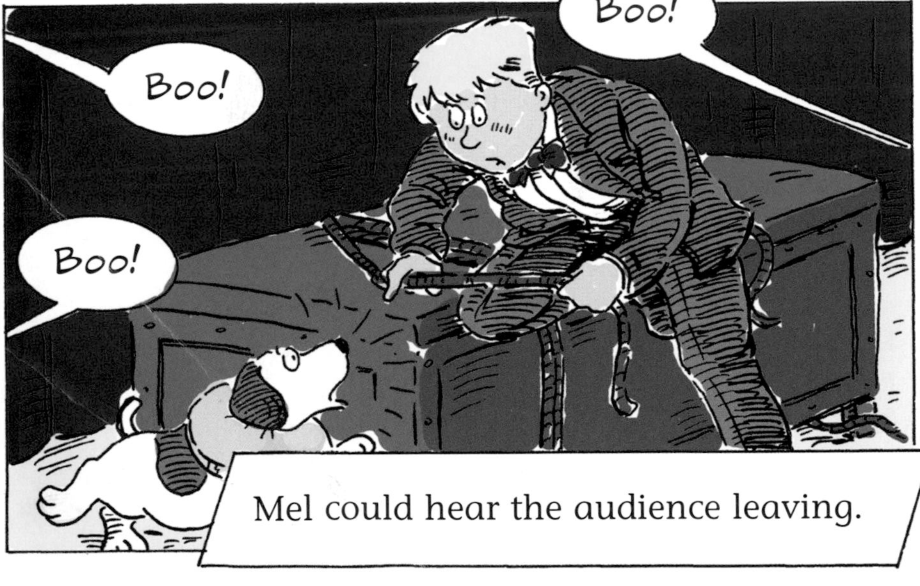
Boo!
Boo!
Boo!
Mel could hear the audience leaving.

Mel managed to open the lid of the steel trunk and saw his father's pale face inside.

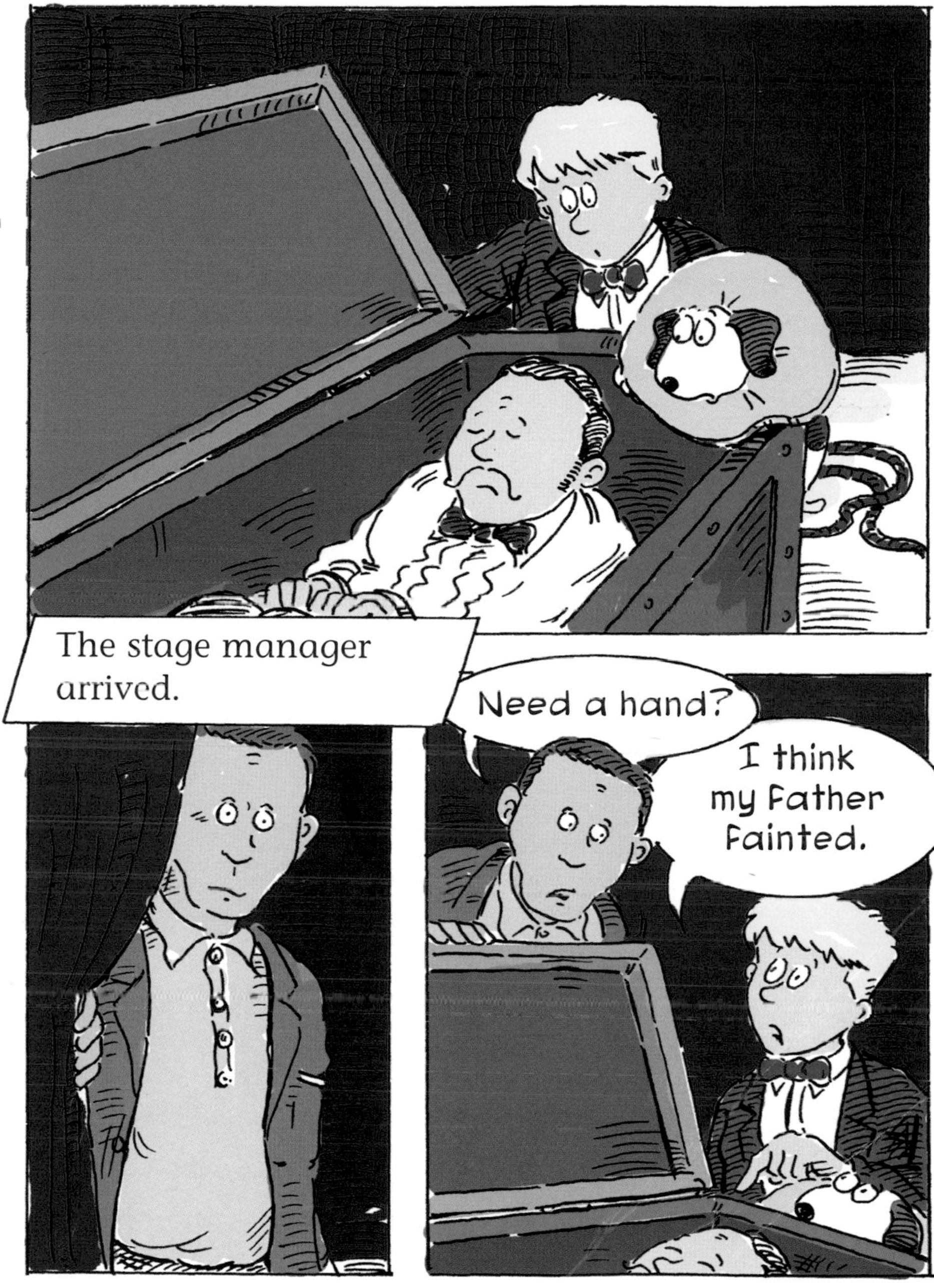
The stage manager arrived.
Need a hand?
I think my father fainted.

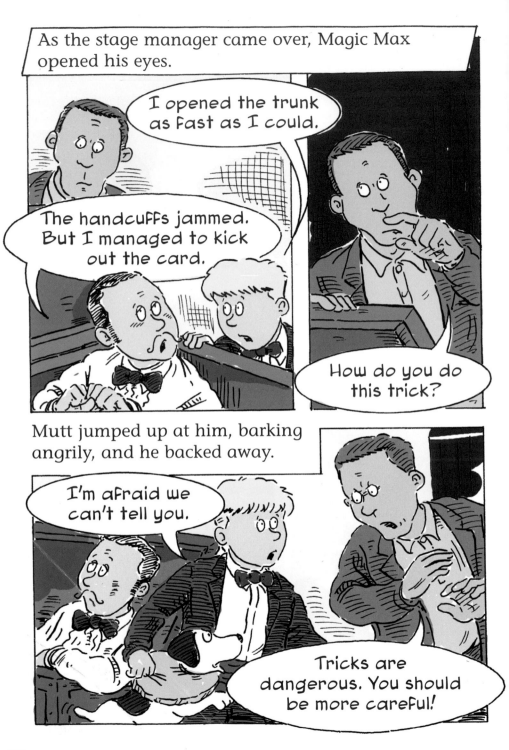

As the stage manager came over, Magic Max opened his eyes.

I opened the trunk as fast as I could.

The handcuffs jammed. But I managed to kick out the card.

How do you do this trick?

Mutt jumped up at him, barking angrily, and he backed away.

I'm afraid we can't tell you.

Tricks are dangerous. You should be more careful!

At home that night, Mel's father seemed to have recovered, but he was very restless.

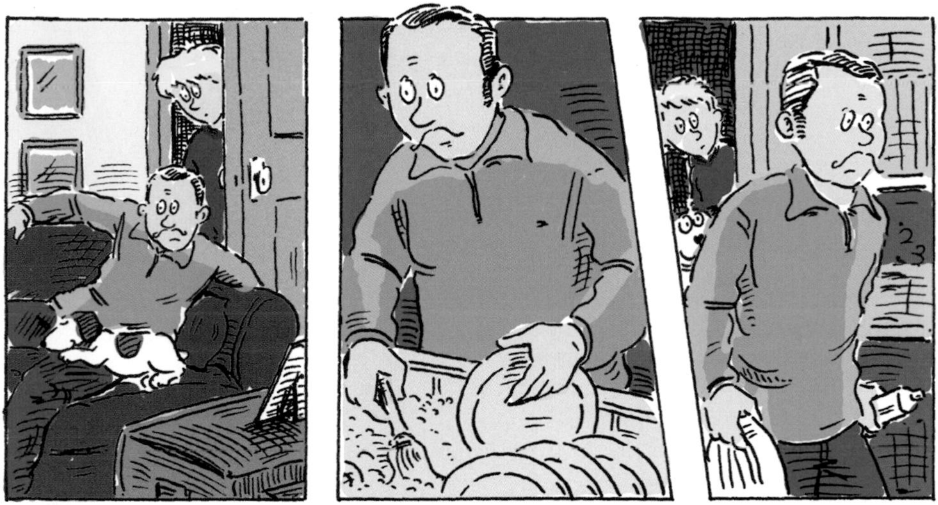

He'd start one chore and then move on to another before finishing the first.

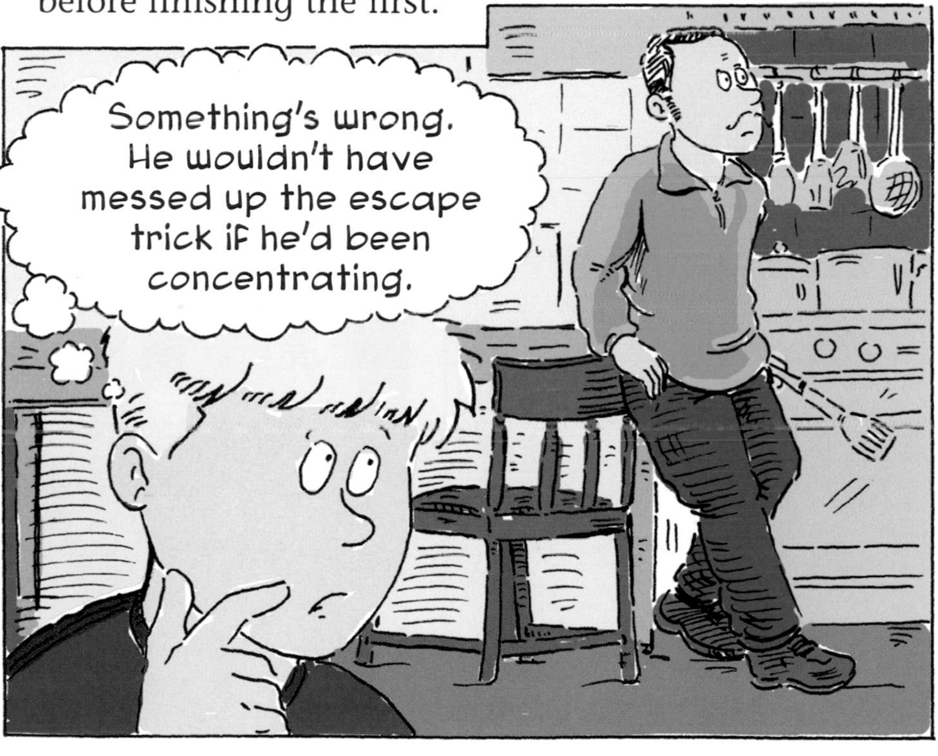
Something's wrong. He wouldn't have messed up the escape trick if he'd been concentrating.

After supper, Mel saw his dad reading a story in the newspaper. Looking over his shoulder, Mel read the caption next to the photo.

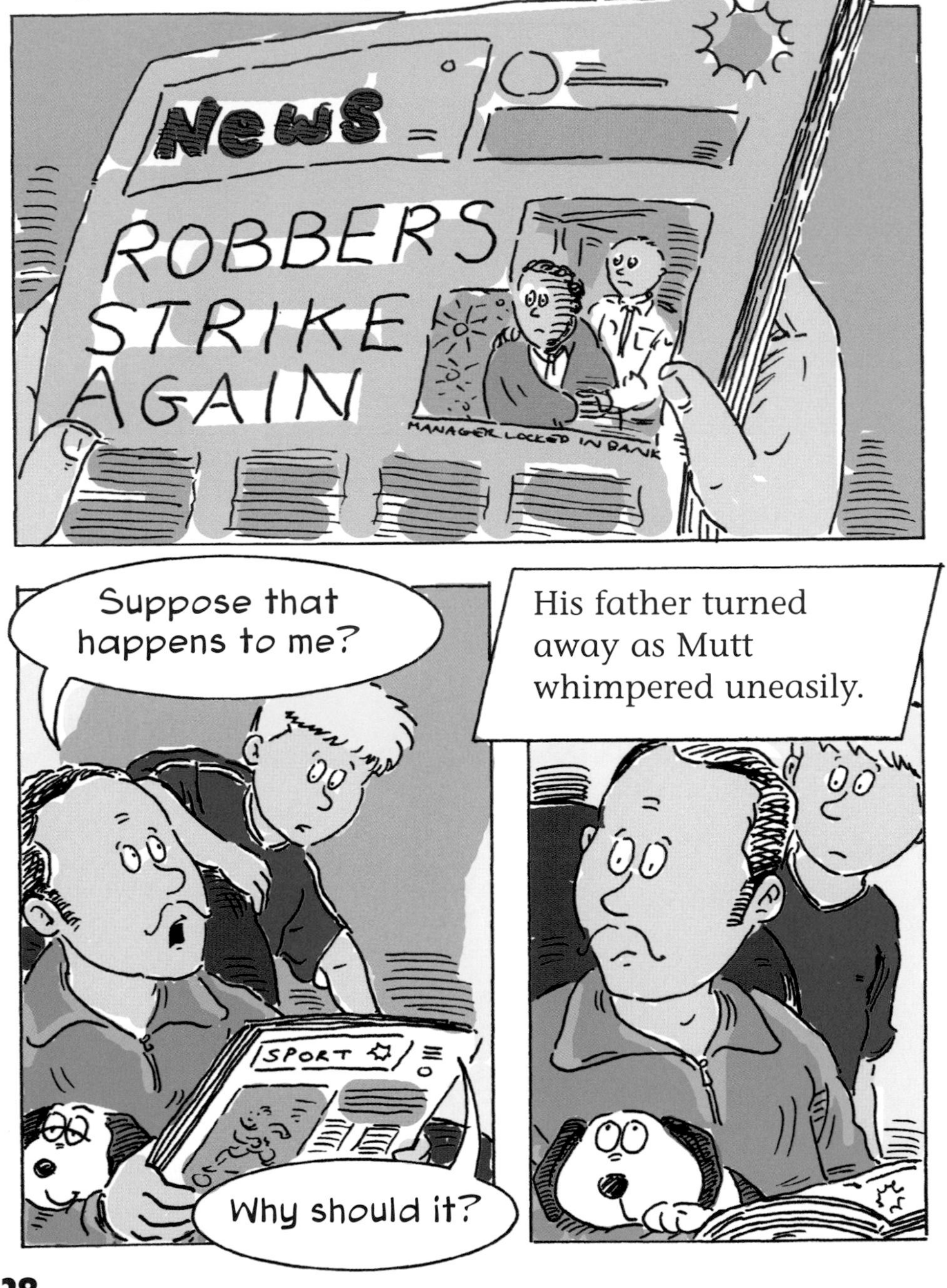
News
ROBBERS STRIKE AGAIN
MANAGER LOCKED IN BANK
Suppose that happens to me?
His father turned away as Mutt whimpered uneasily.
SPORT
Why should it?

CHAPTER FOUR

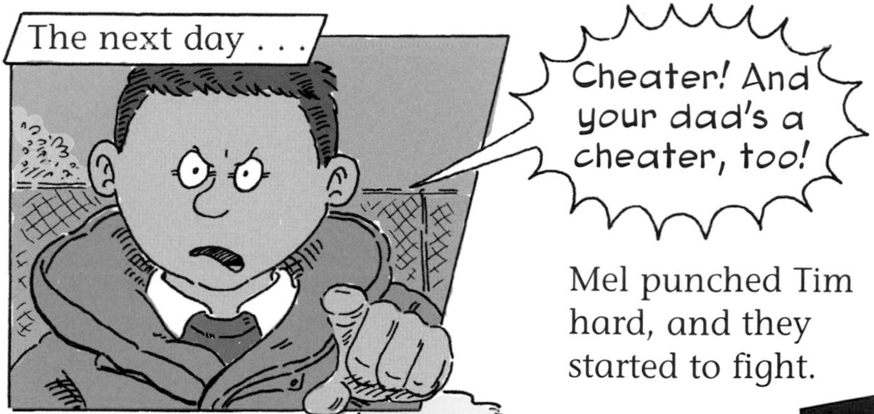
The next day . . .
Cheater! And your dad's a cheater, too!

Mel punched Tim hard, and they started to fight.

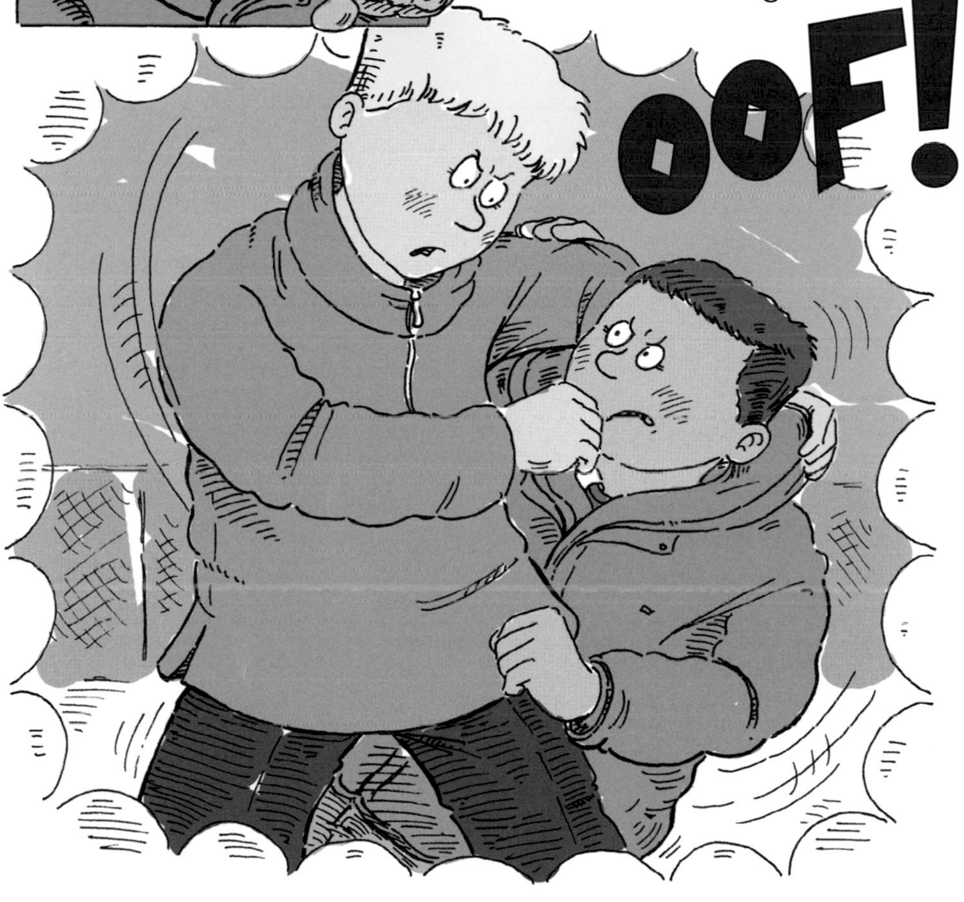
OOF!

Finally Paul and some of their friends pulled them apart.

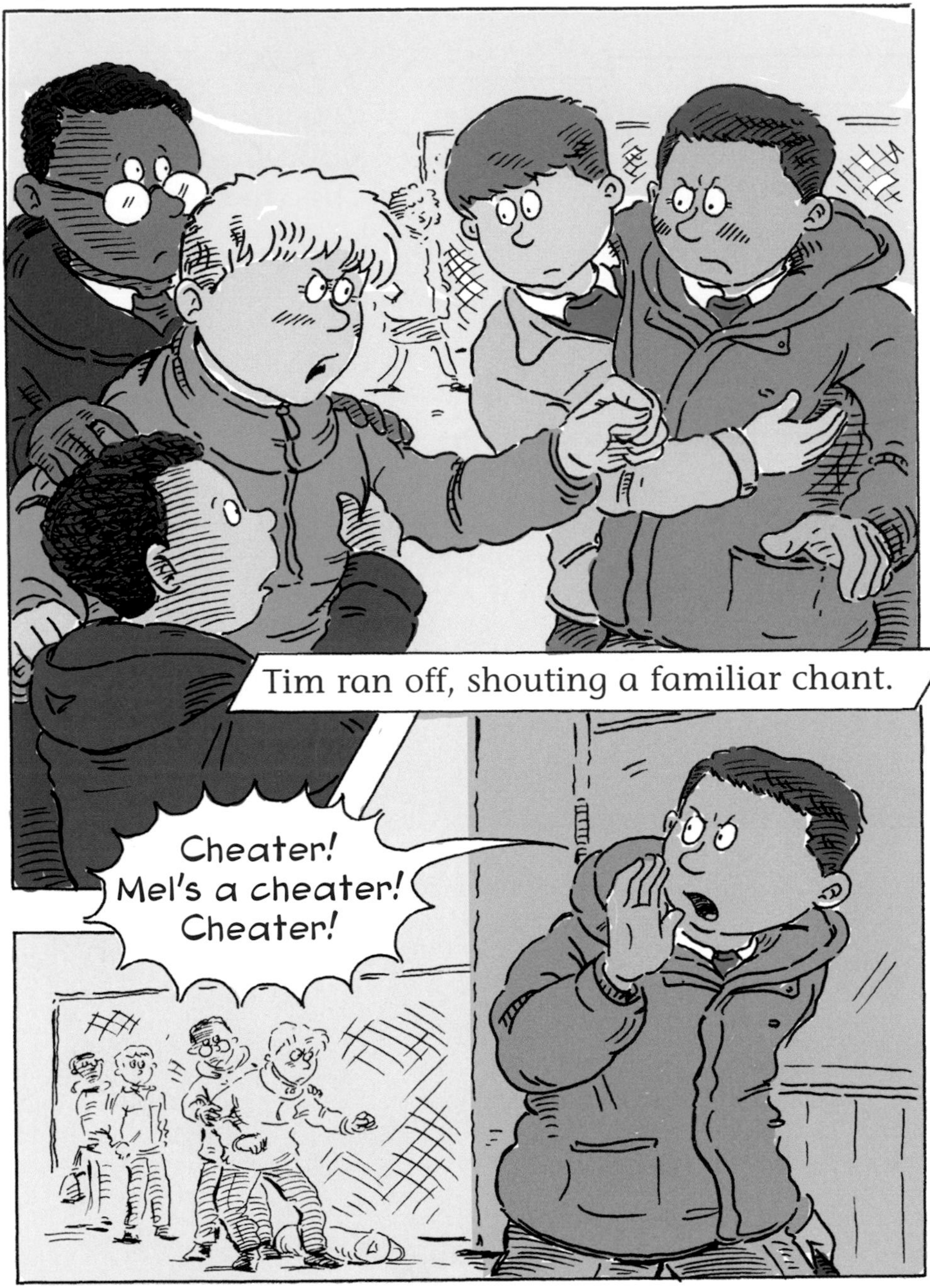
Tim ran off, shouting a familiar chant.
Cheater! Mel's a cheater! Cheater!

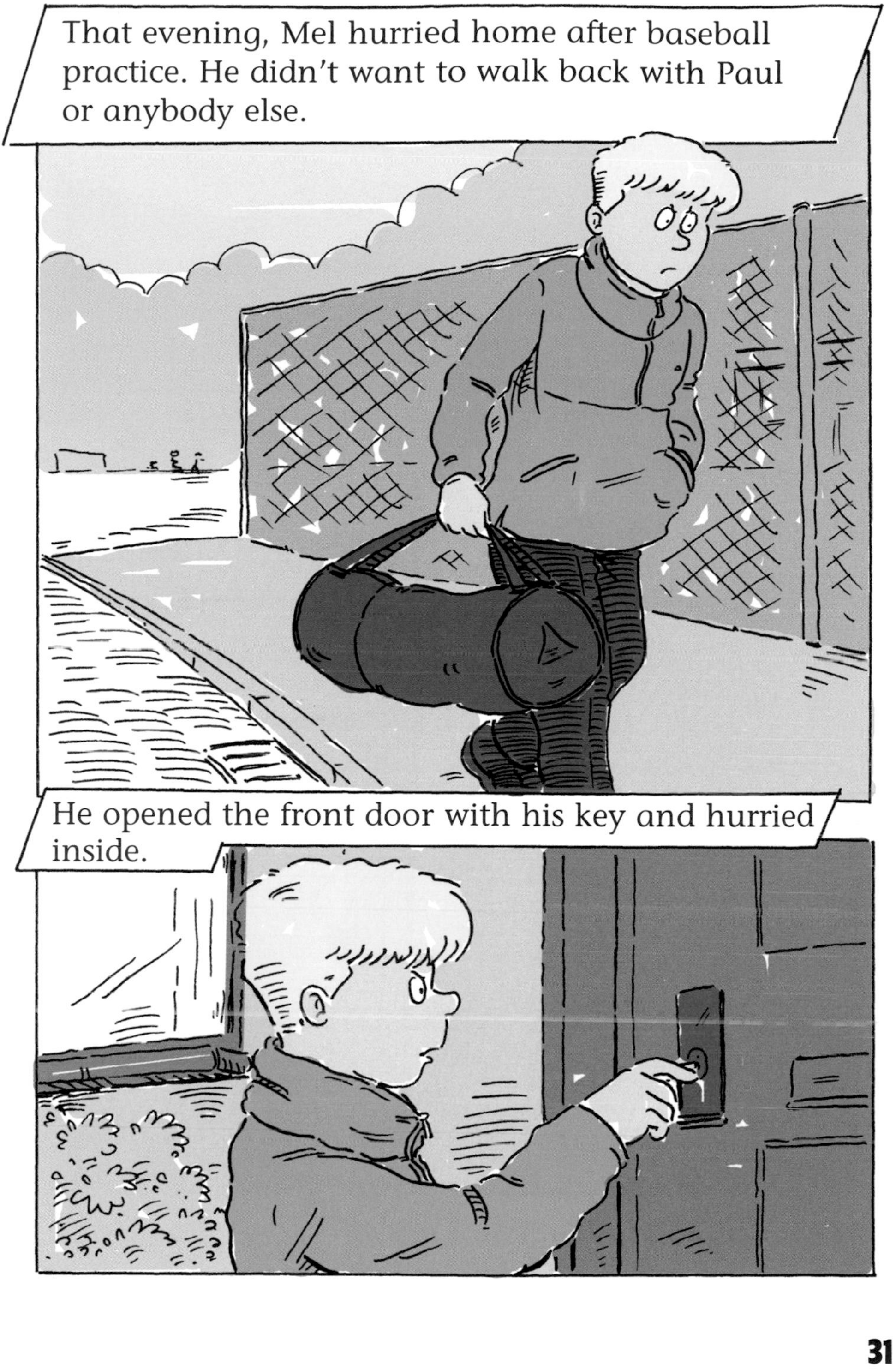
That evening, Mel hurried home after baseball practice. He didn't want to walk back with Paul or anybody else.
He opened the front door with his key and hurried inside.

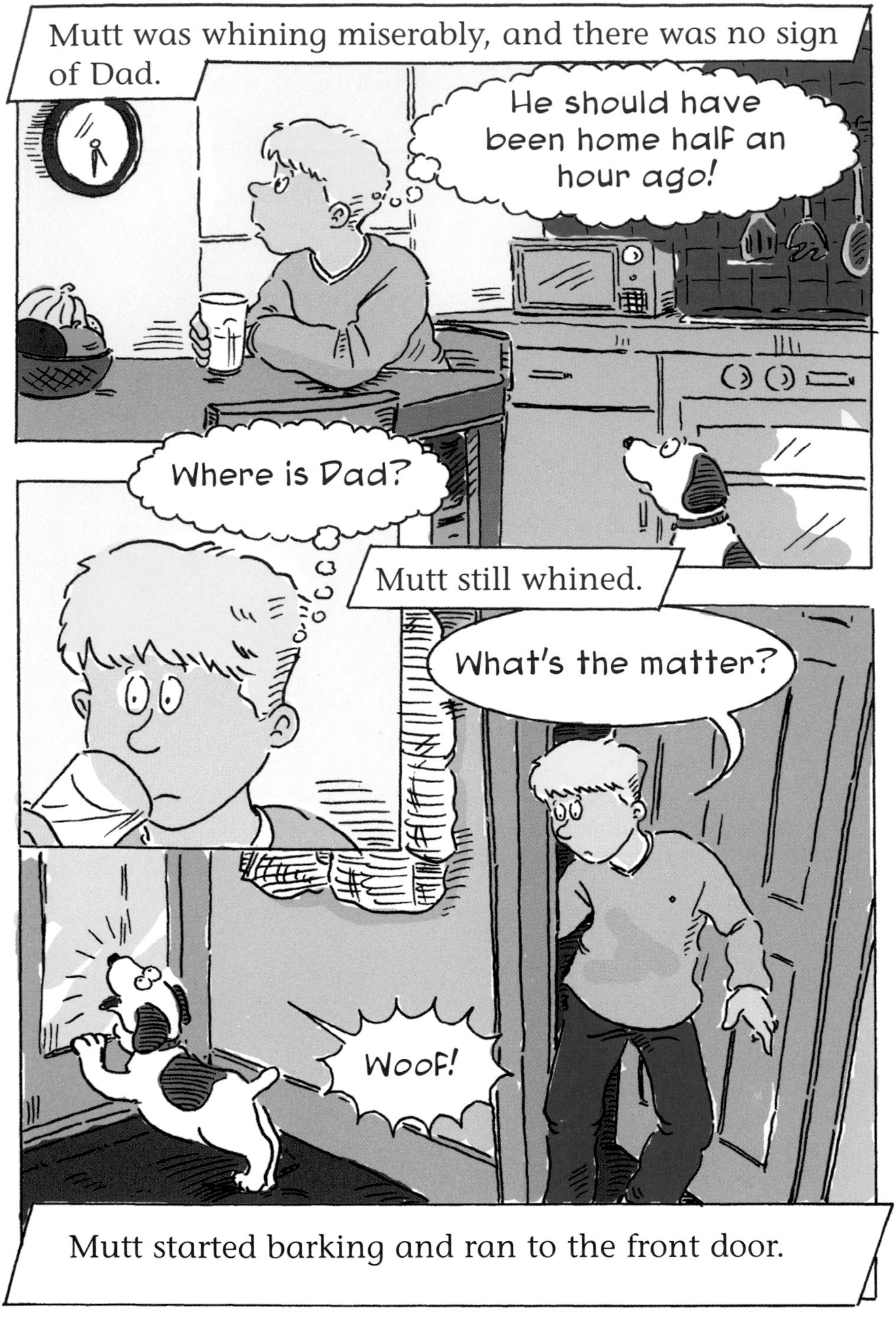
Mutt was whining miserably, and there was no sign of Dad.
He should have been home half an hour ago!
Where is Dad?
Mutt still whined.
What's the matter?
Woof!
Mutt started barking and ran to the front door.

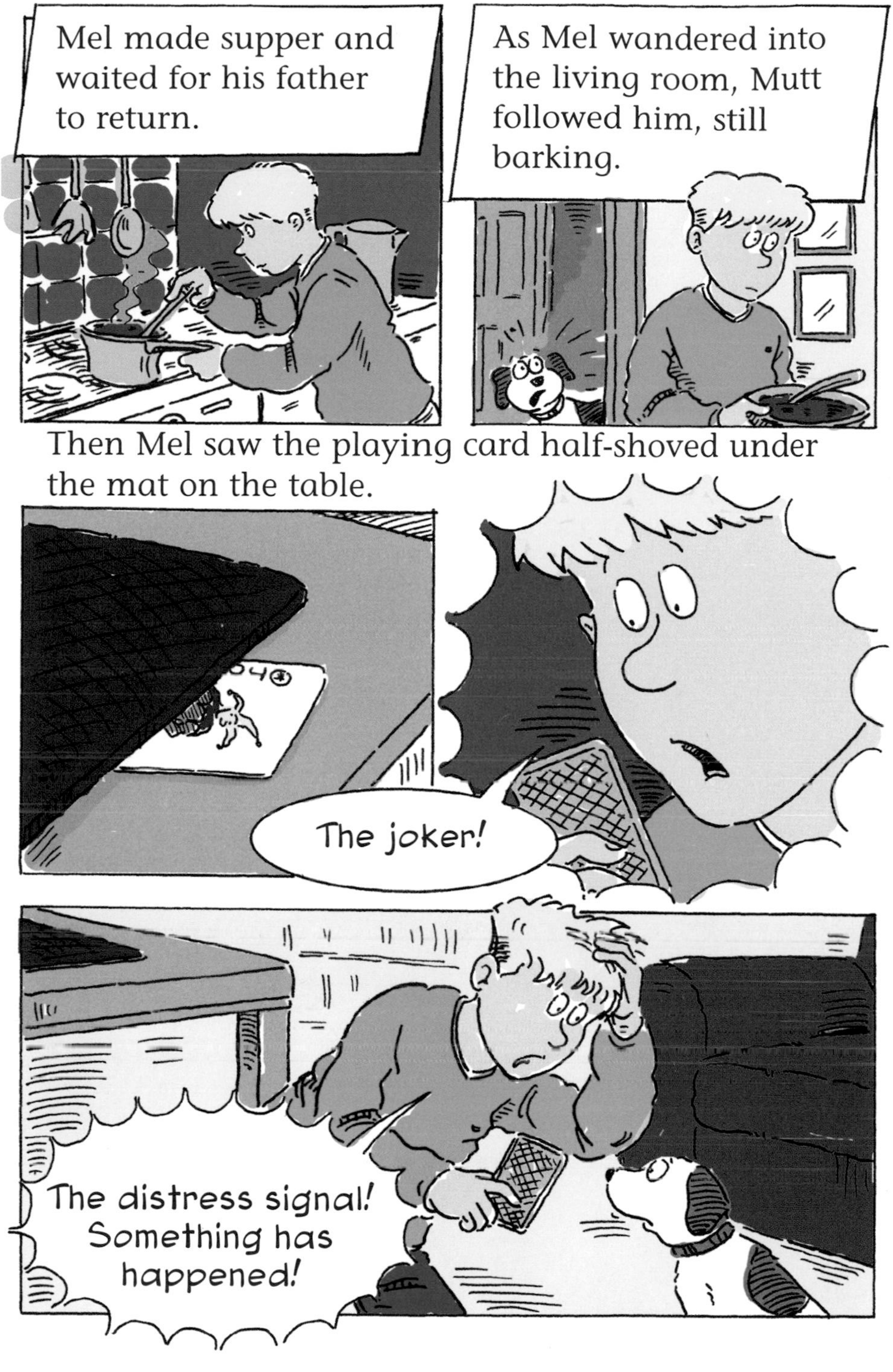
Mel made supper and waited for his father to return.
As Mel wandered into the living room, Mutt followed him, still barking.
Then Mel saw the playing card half-shoved under the mat on the table.
The joker!
The distress signal! Something has happened!

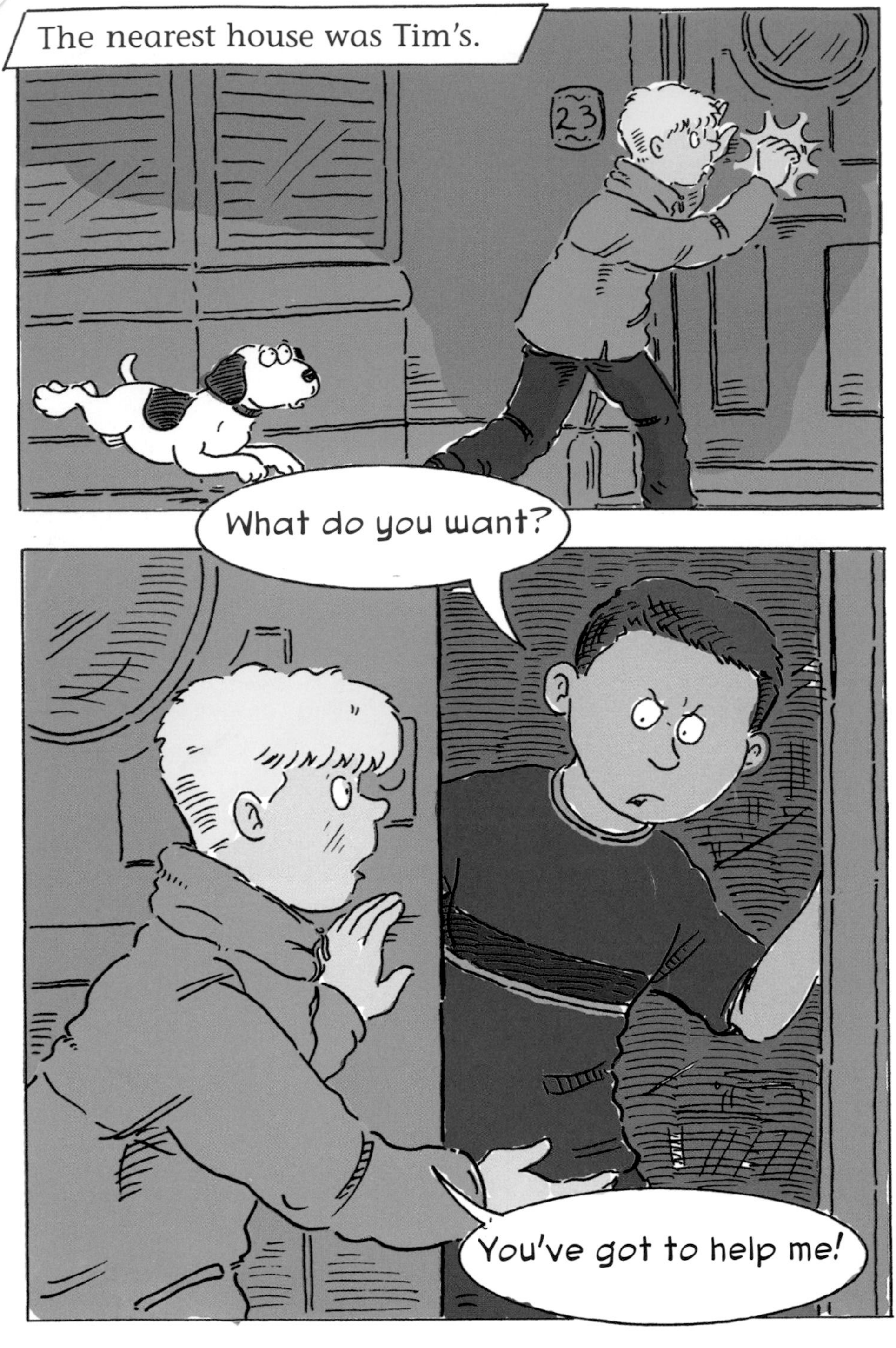
The nearest house was Tim's.
23
What do you want?
You've got to help me!

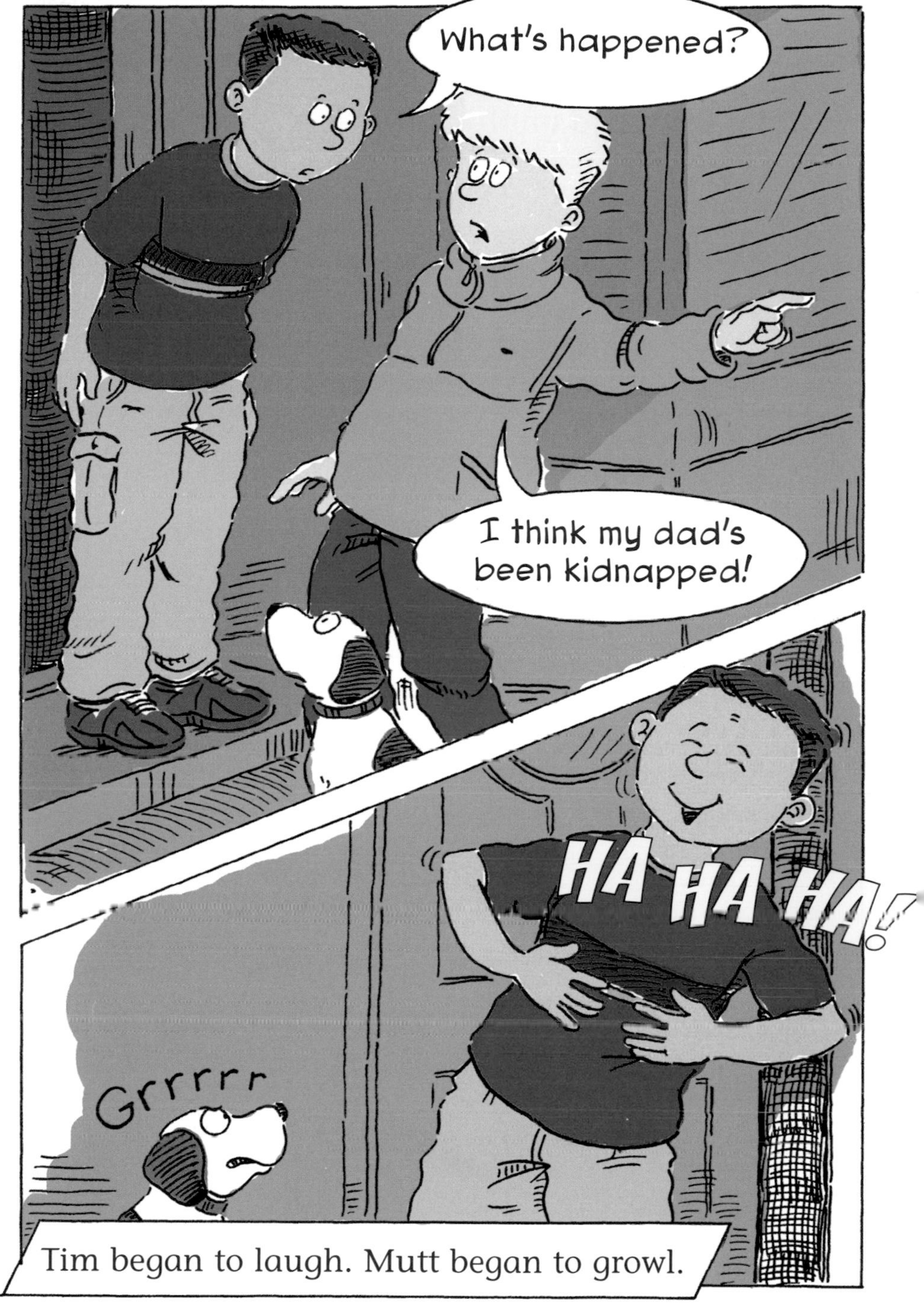
What's happened?
I think my dad's been kidnapped!
HA HA HA!
Grrrrr
Tim began to laugh. Mutt began to growl.

Mel ran down the road to Paul's house, followed by Mutt.

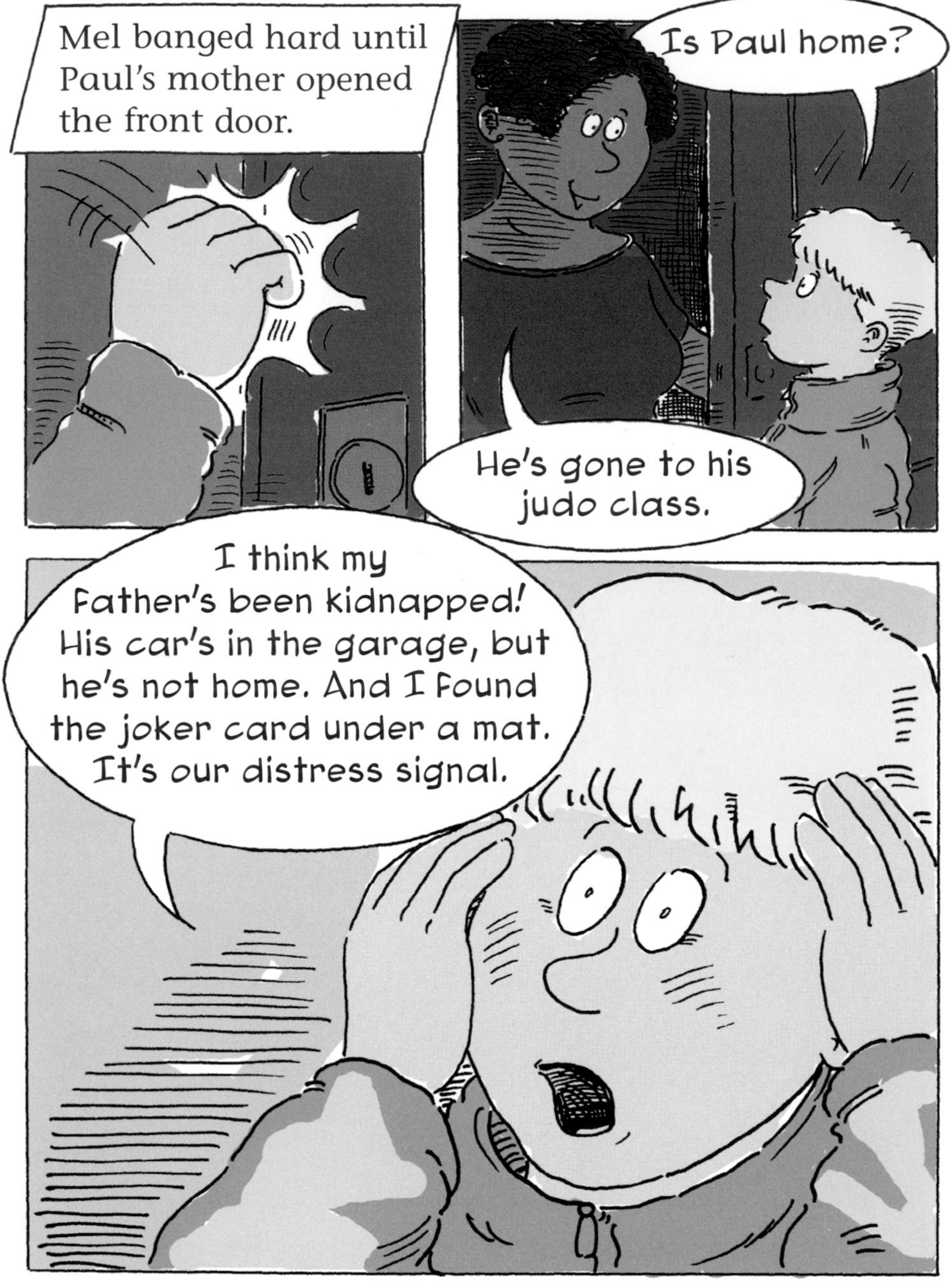
Mel banged hard until Paul's mother opened the front door.
Is Paul home?
He's gone to his judo class.
I think my Father's been kidnapped! His car's in the garage, but he's not home. And I found the joker card under a mat. It's our distress signal.

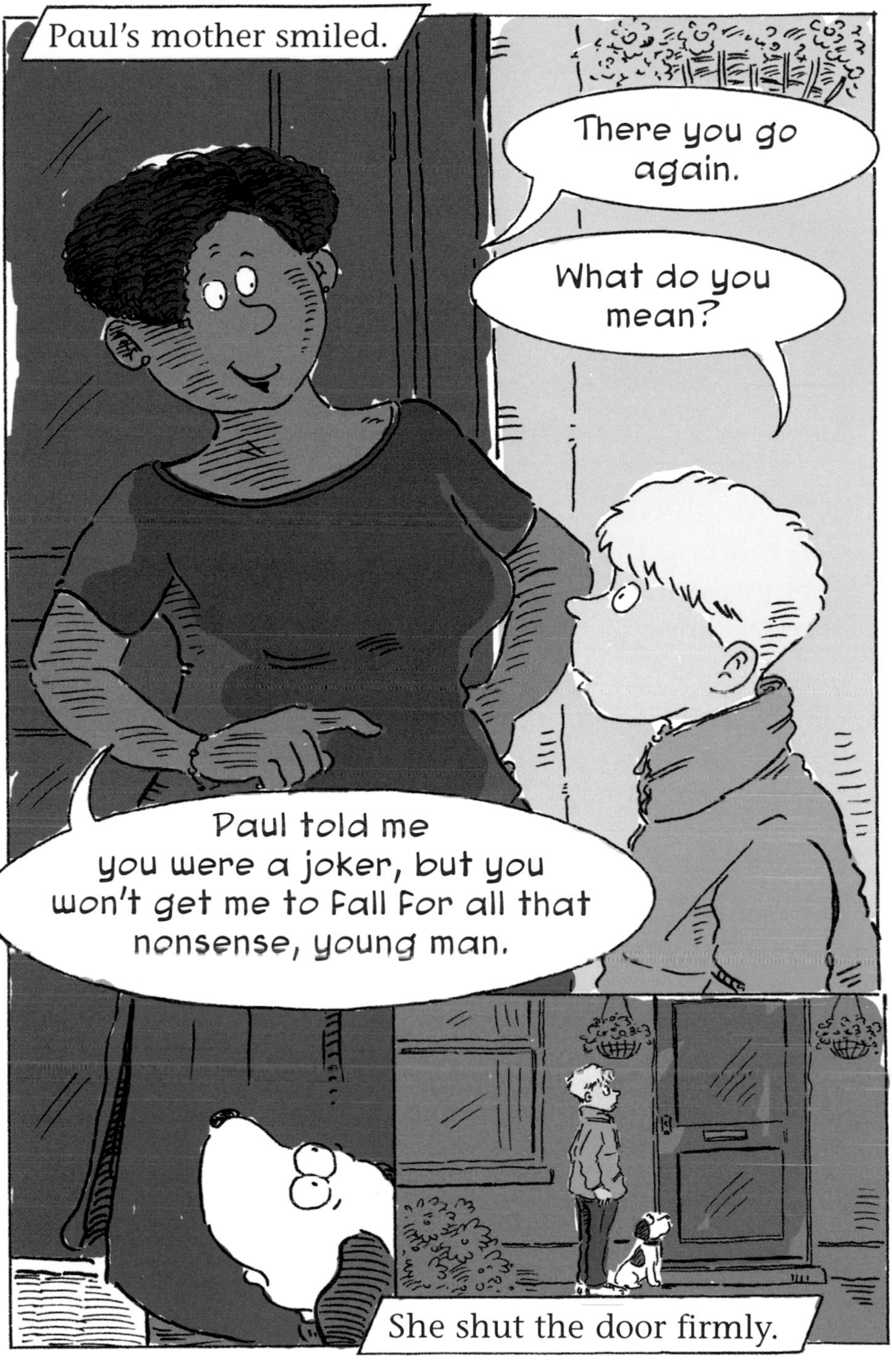
Paul's mother smiled.
There you go again.
What do you mean?
Paul told me you were a joker, but you won't get me to fall for all that nonsense, young man.
She shut the door firmly.

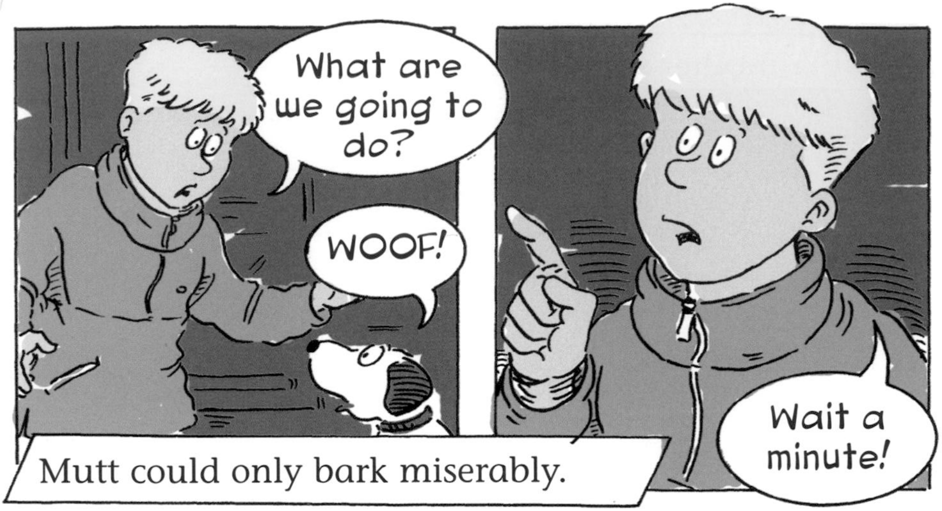
What are we going to do?
WOOF!
Mutt could only bark miserably.
Wait a minute!

Mel remembered how his dad had been reading the newspaper the other evening.

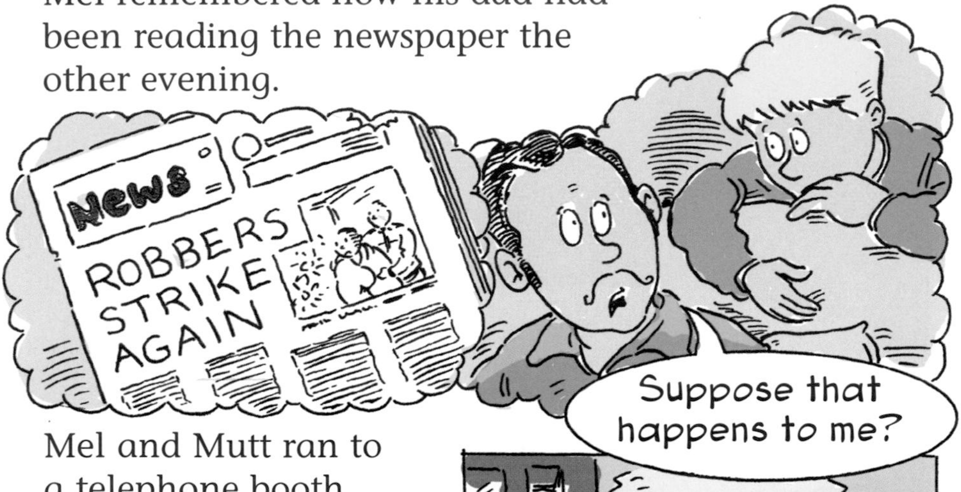
News
ROBBERS STRIKE AGAIN
Suppose that happens to me?

Mel and Mutt ran to a telephone booth.

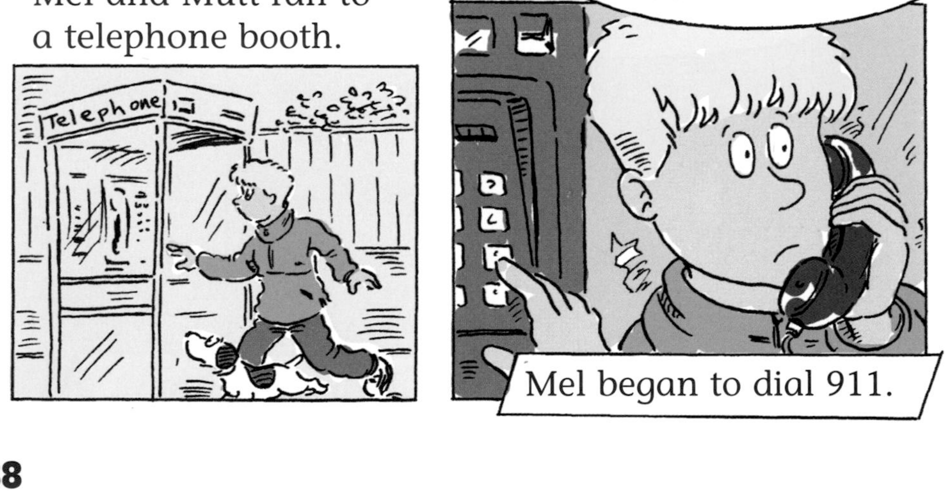
Telephone
Mel began to dial 911.

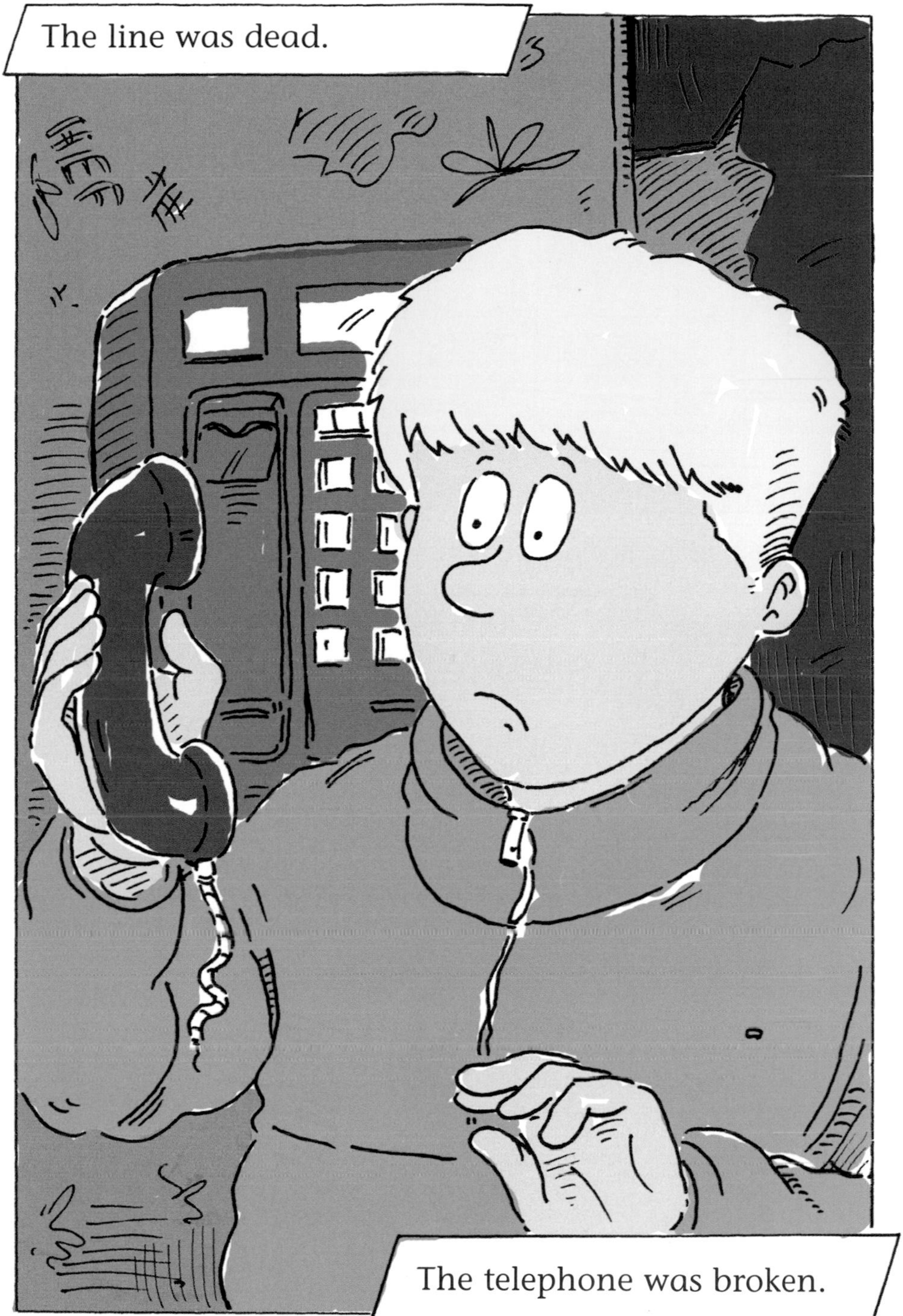
The line was dead.
The telephone was broken.

CHAPTER FIVE

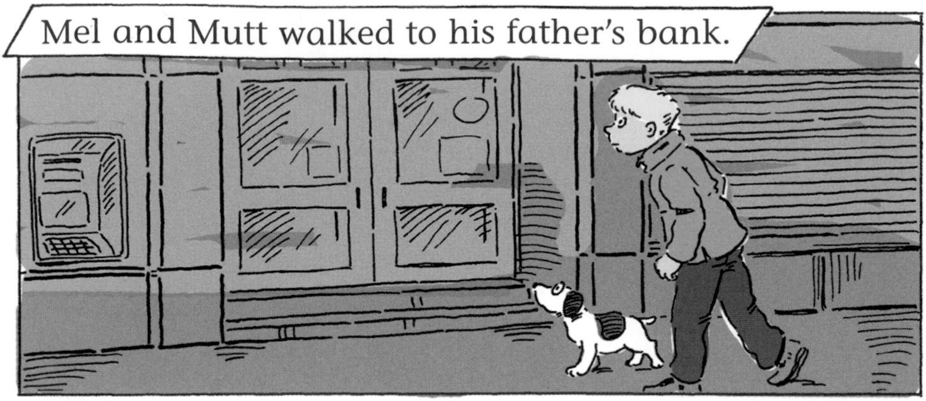
Mel and Mutt walked to his father's bank.

It was just after 8 o'clock. The street was dark and silent.

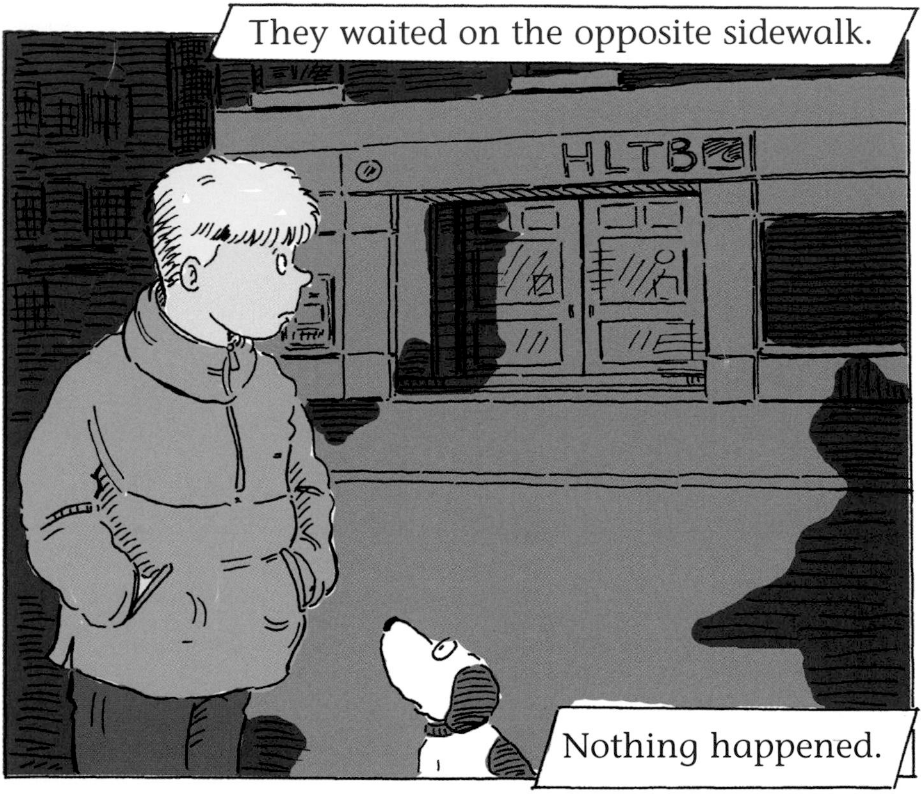
They waited on the opposite sidewalk.
HLTB
Nothing happened.

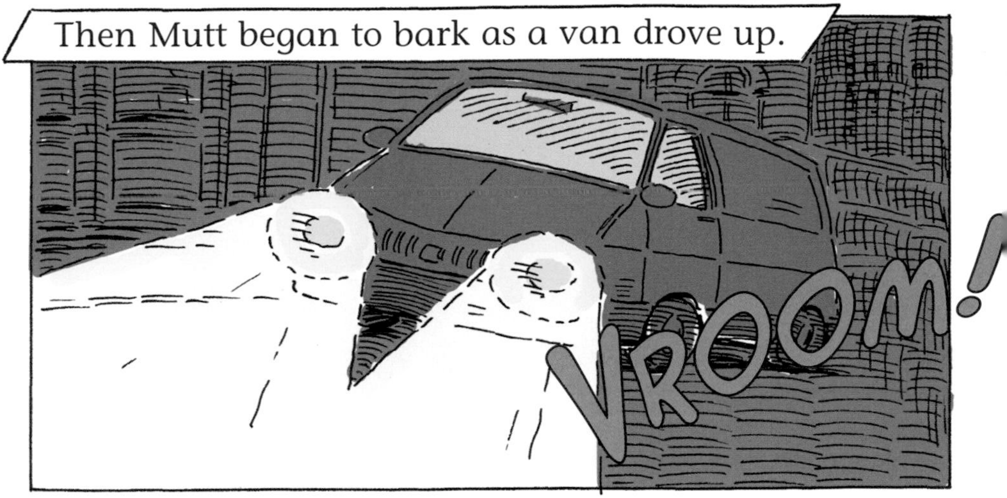
Then Mutt began to bark as a van drove up.
VROOM!

Mel grabbed Mutt and put a hand over his muzzle as they backed into the shadows.

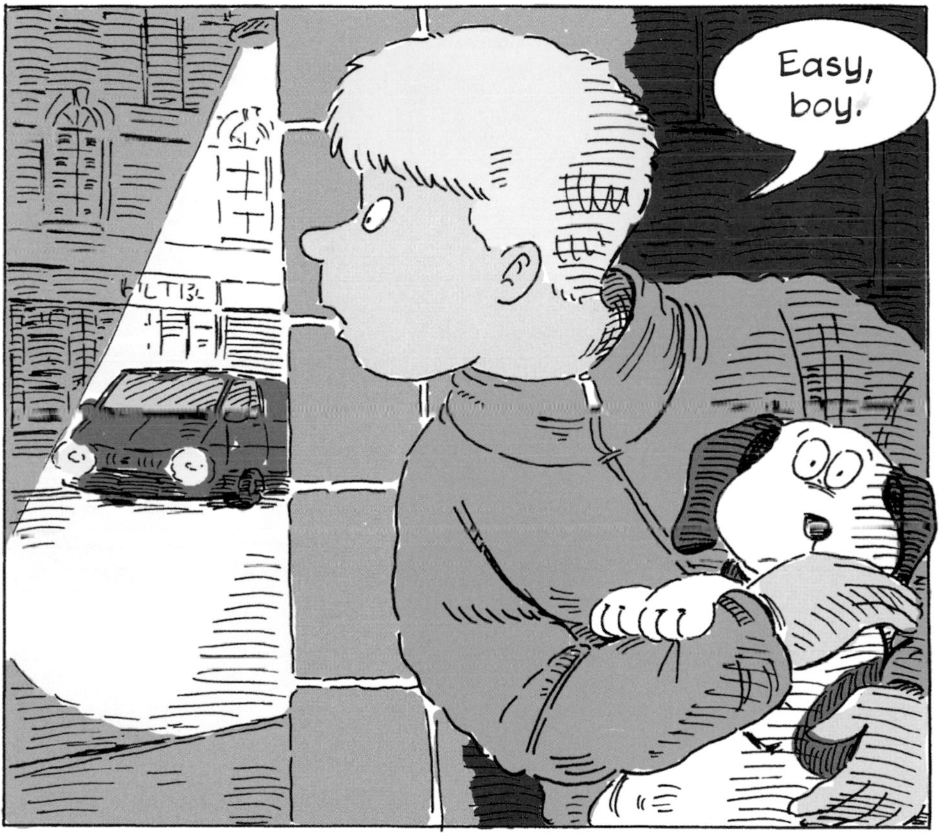
Easy, boy.

The people inside the van seemed to be waiting for something.

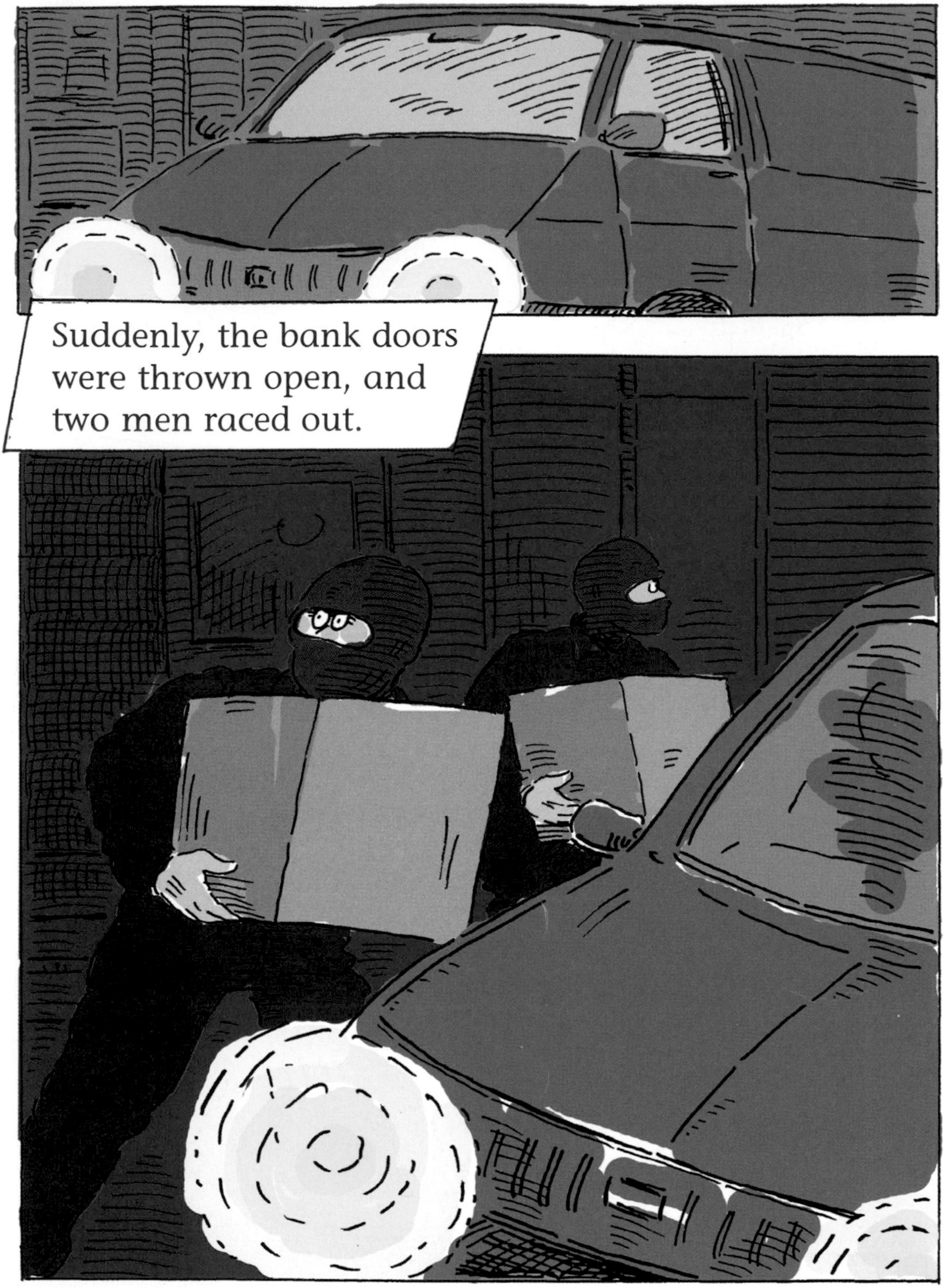
Suddenly, the bank doors were thrown open, and two men raced out.

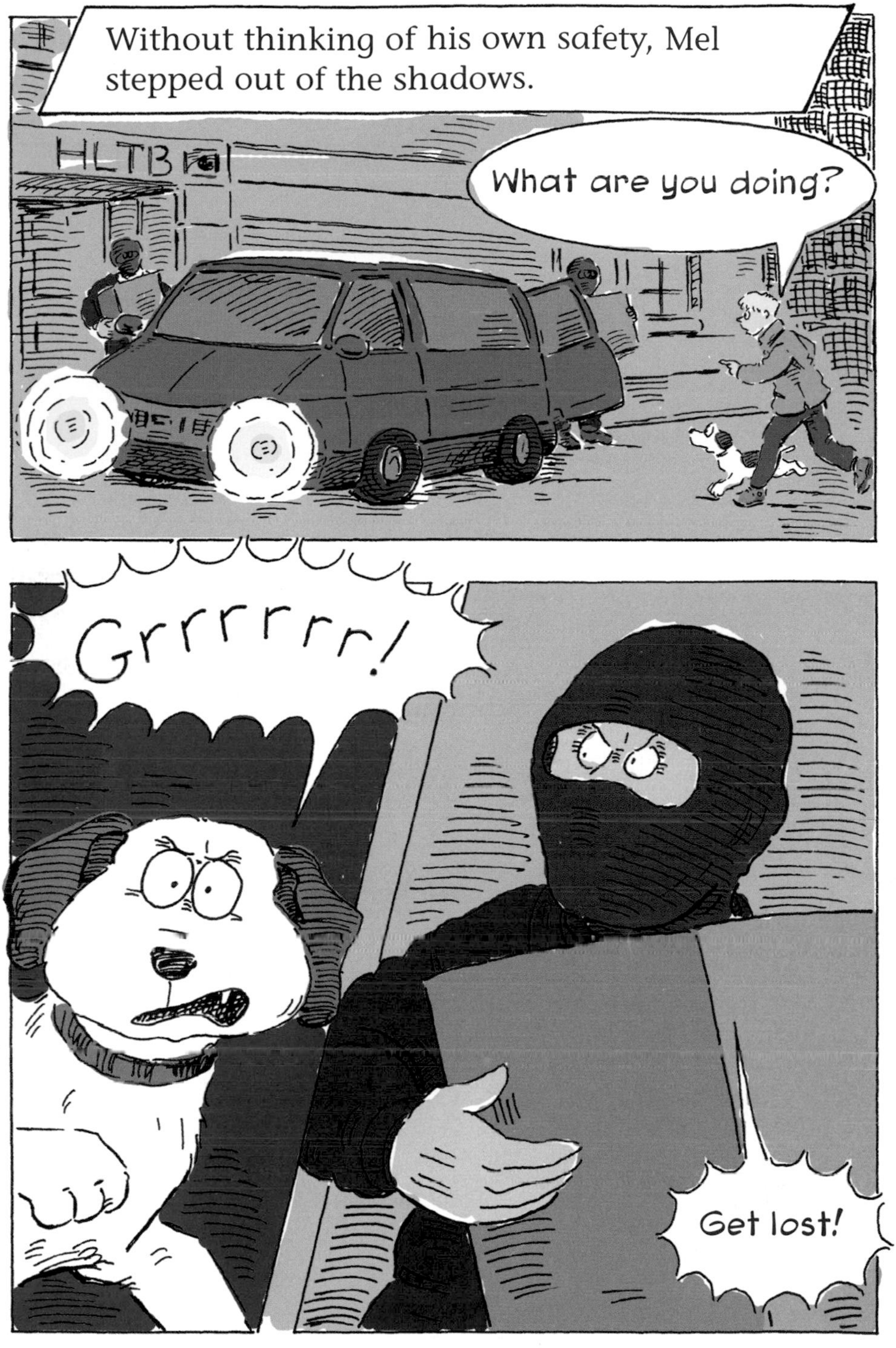
Without thinking of his own safety, Mel stepped out of the shadows.
HLTB
What are you doing?
Grrrrrr!
Get lost!

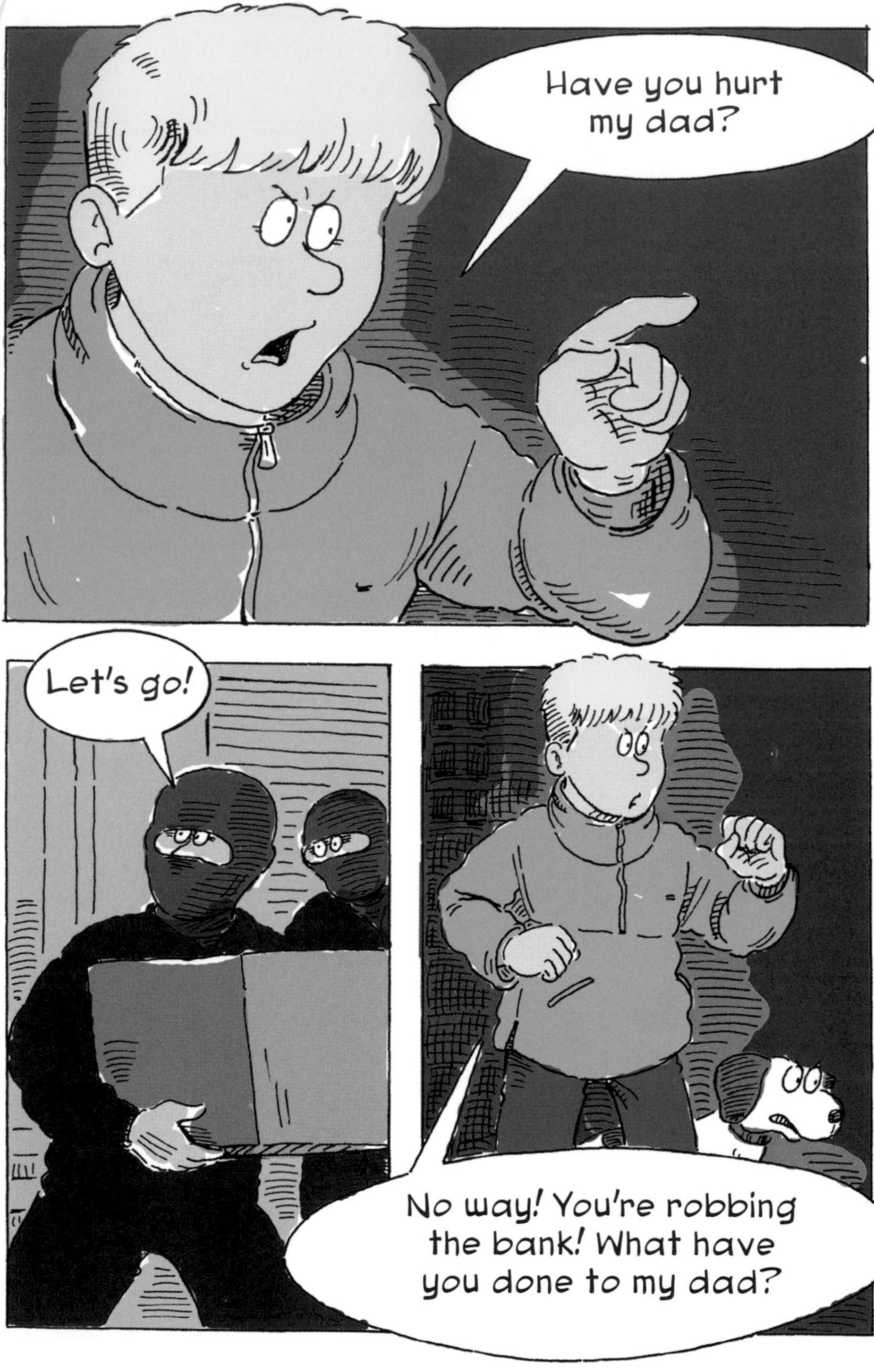
Have you hurt my dad?
Let's go!
No way! You're robbing the bank! What have you done to my dad?

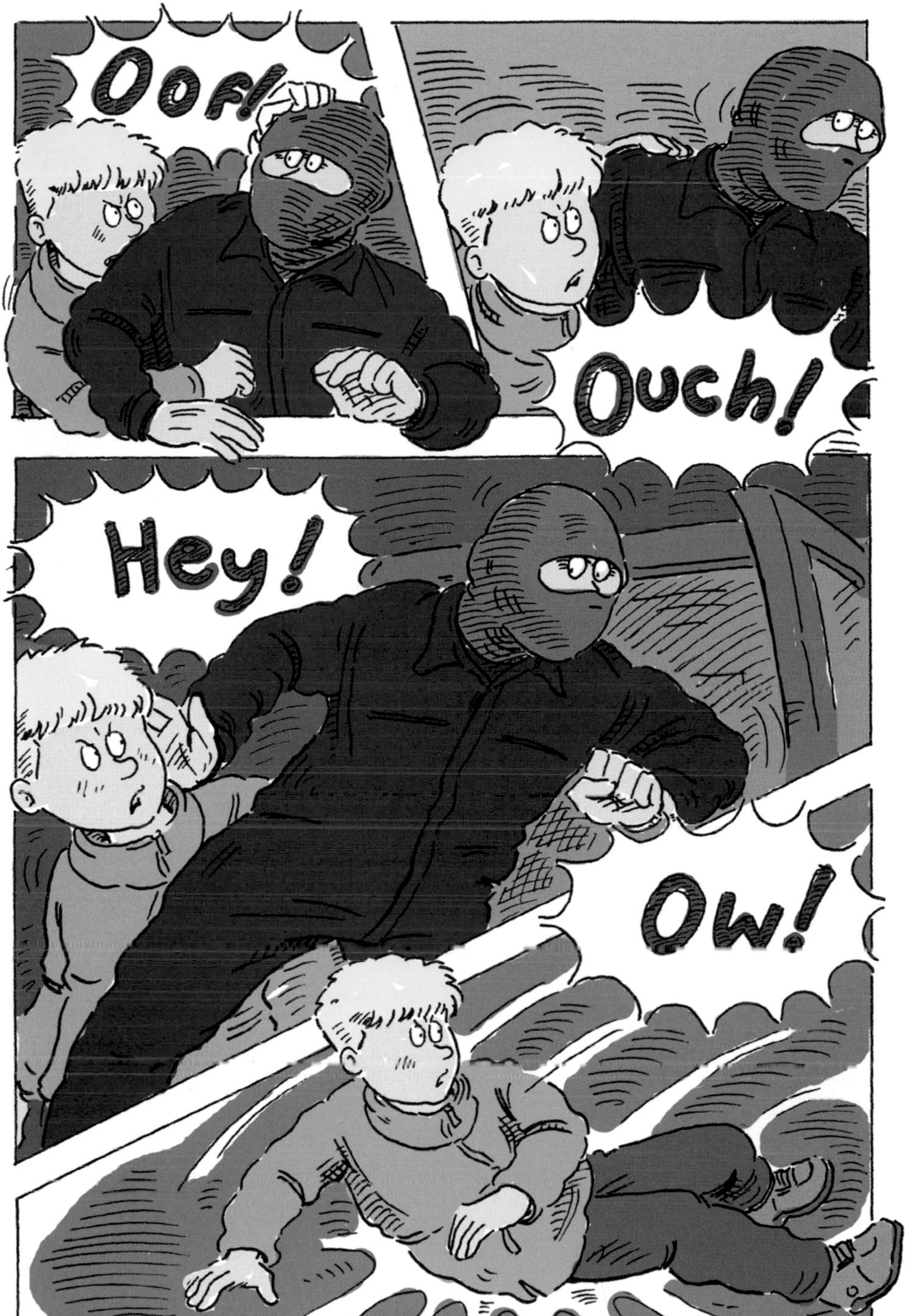
Oof!
Ouch!
Hey!
Ow!

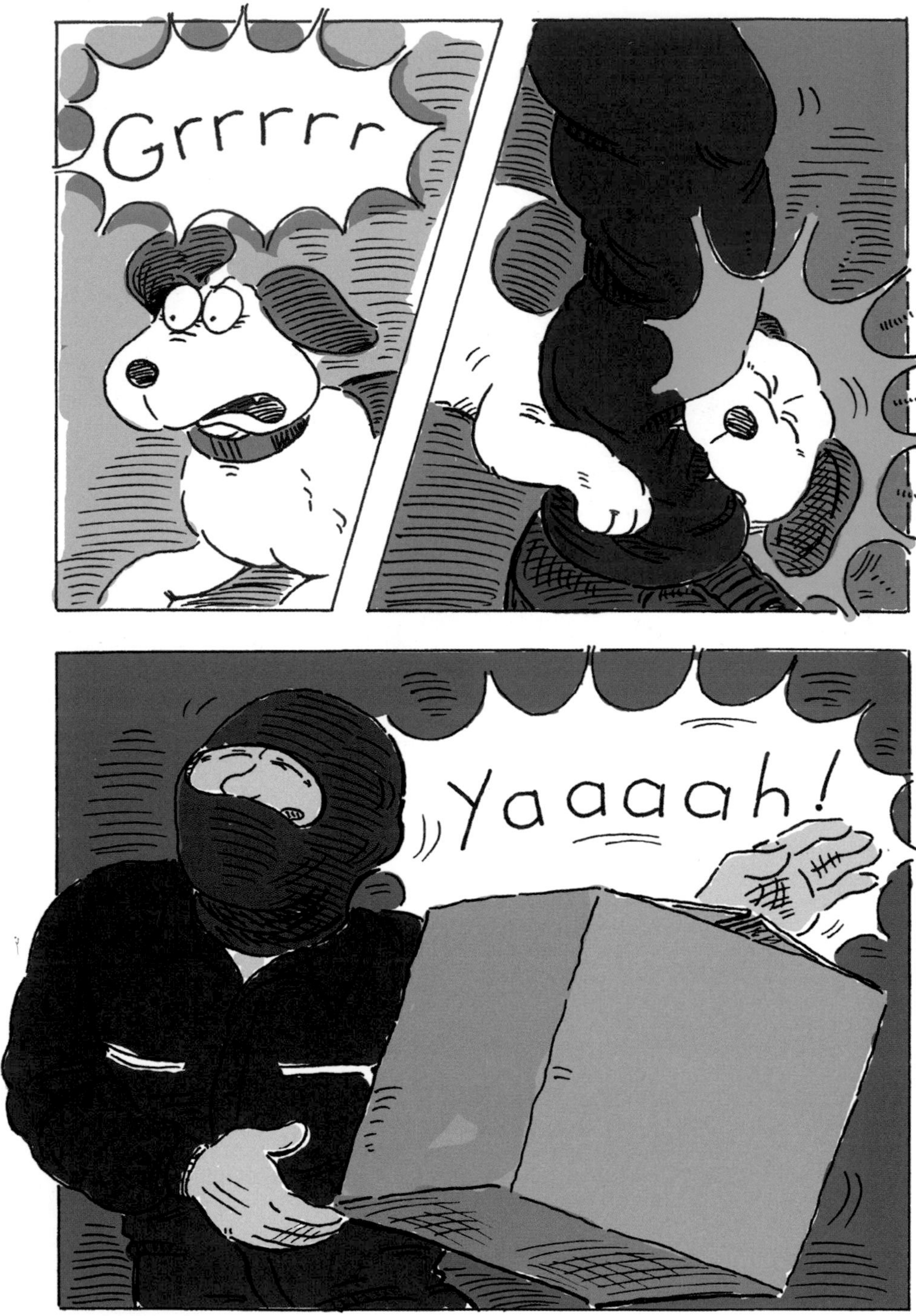
Grrrrr
Yaaaah!

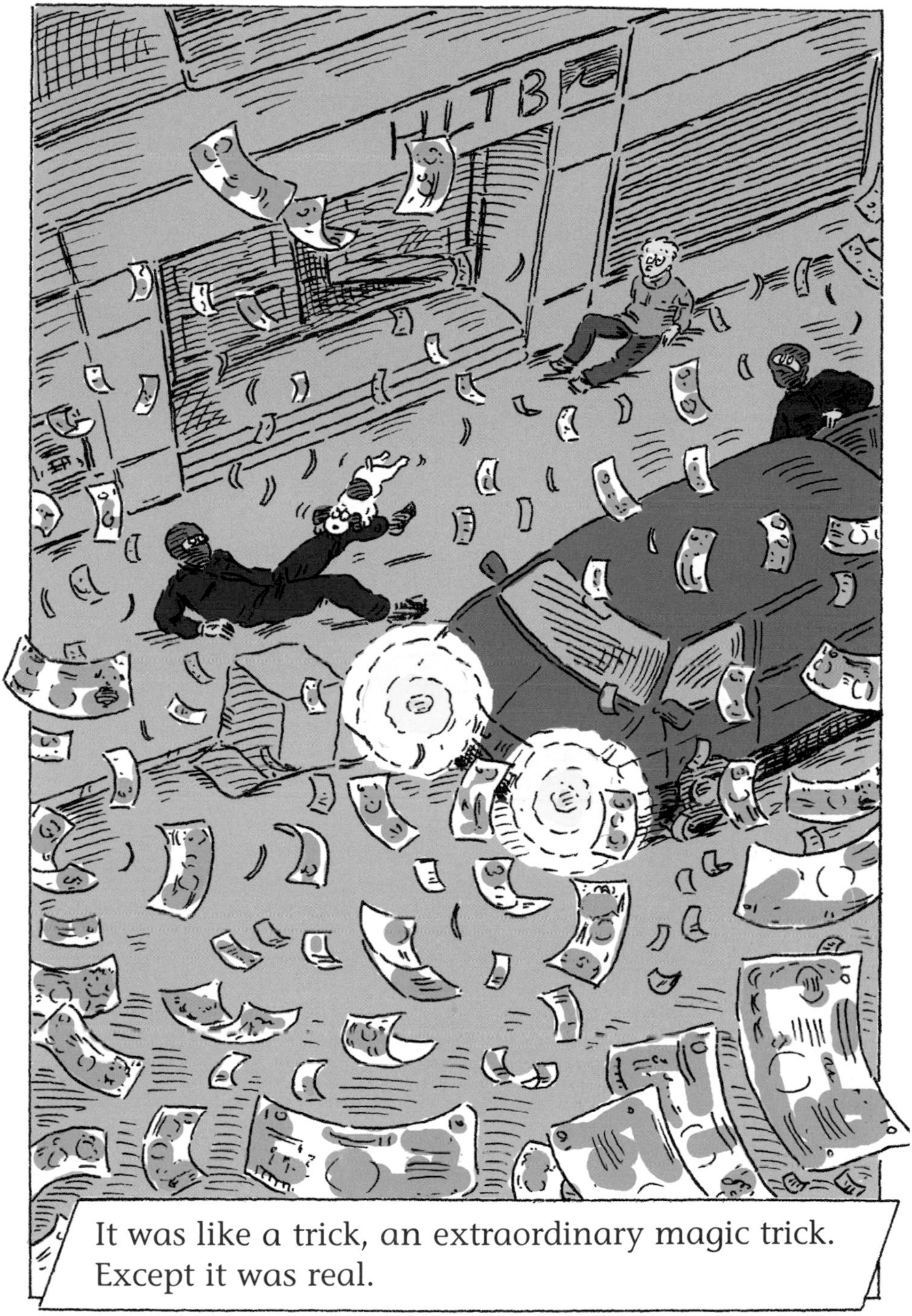
HLTB
It was like a trick, an extraordinary magic trick.
Except it was real.

The robbers began to scramble for the fluttering dollar bills, but Mutt did his best to stop them.

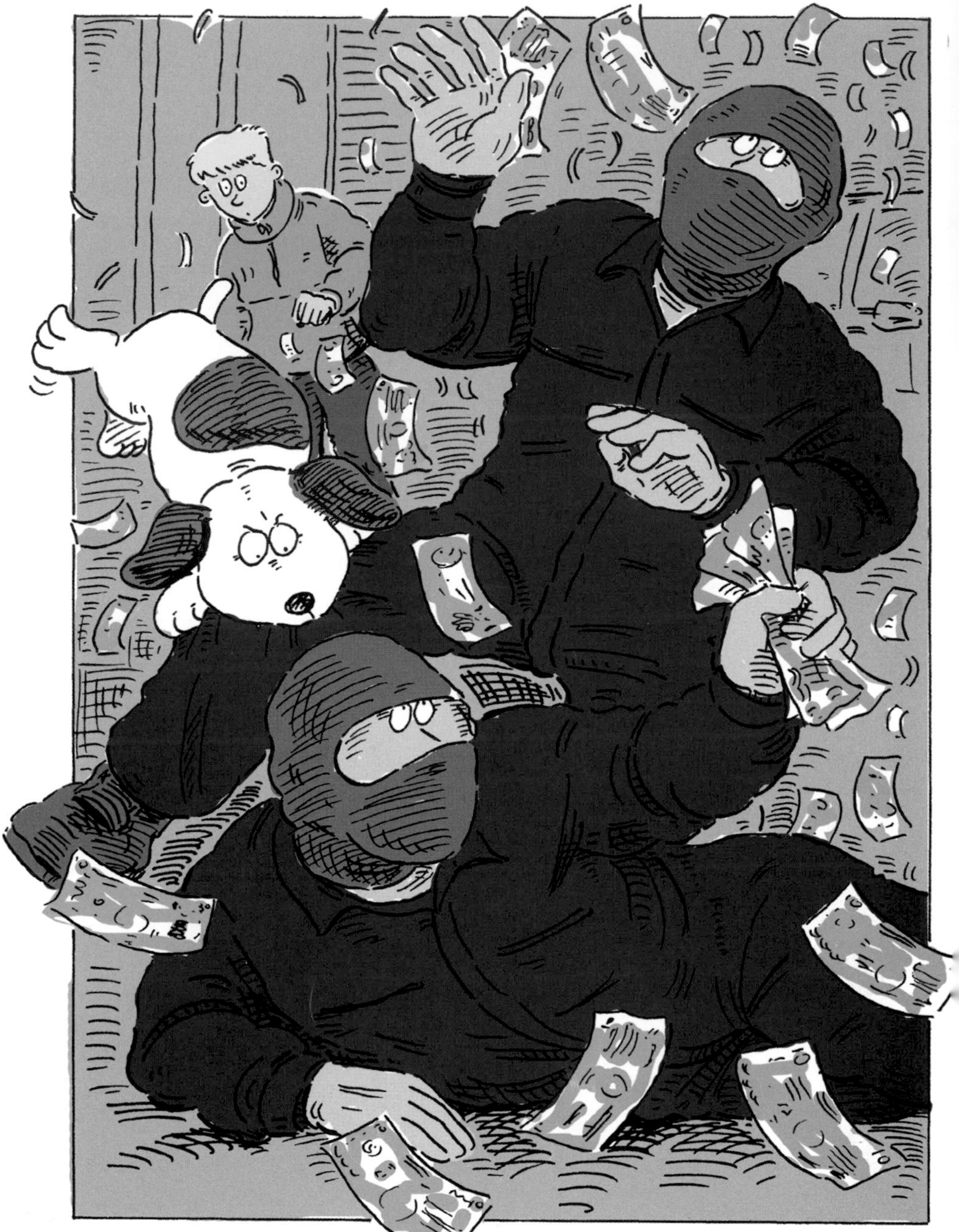

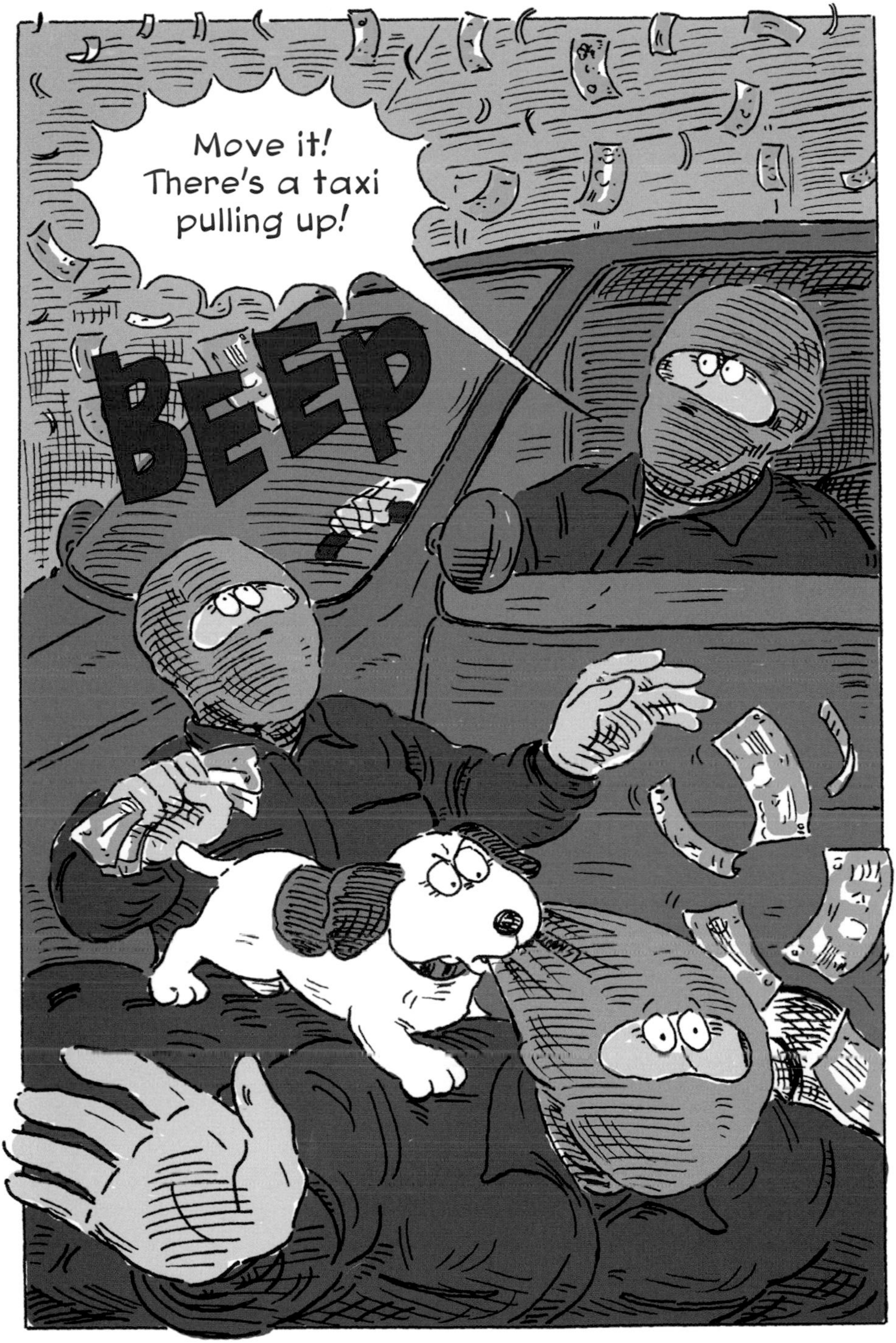
Move it! There's a taxi pulling up!
BEEP

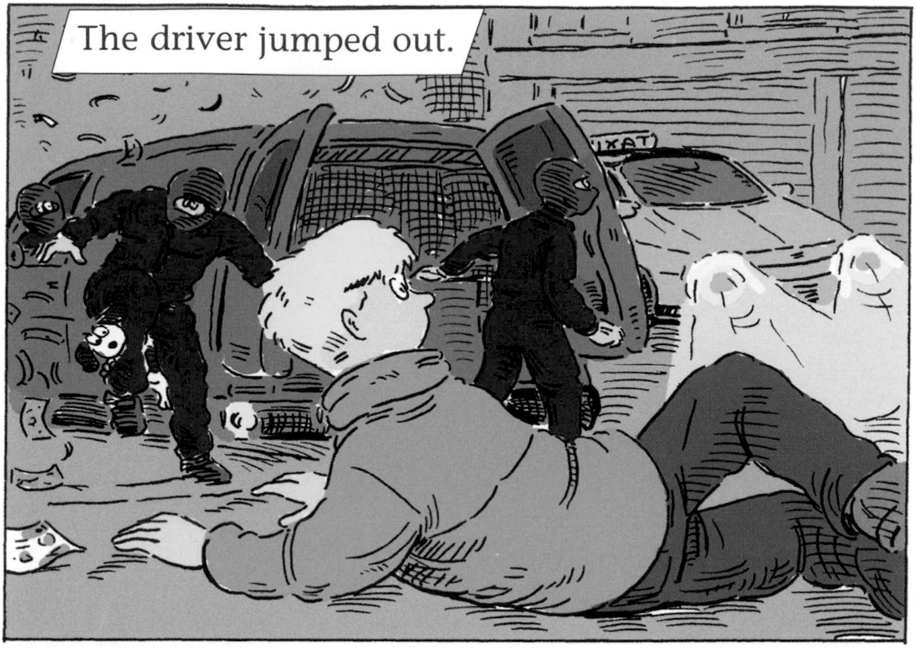
The driver jumped out.
IXAT

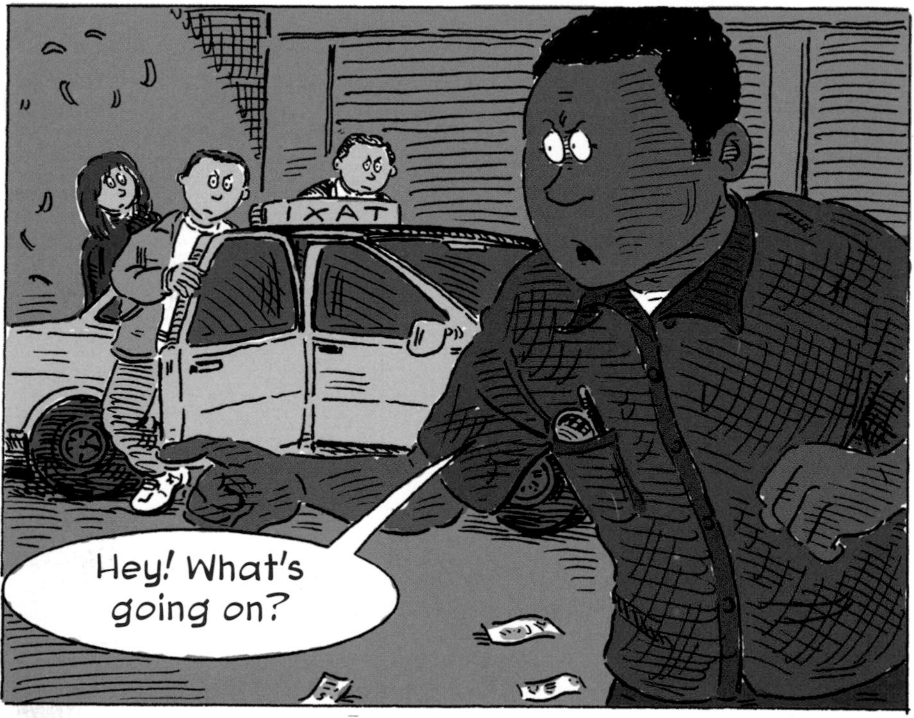
IXAT
Hey! What's going on?

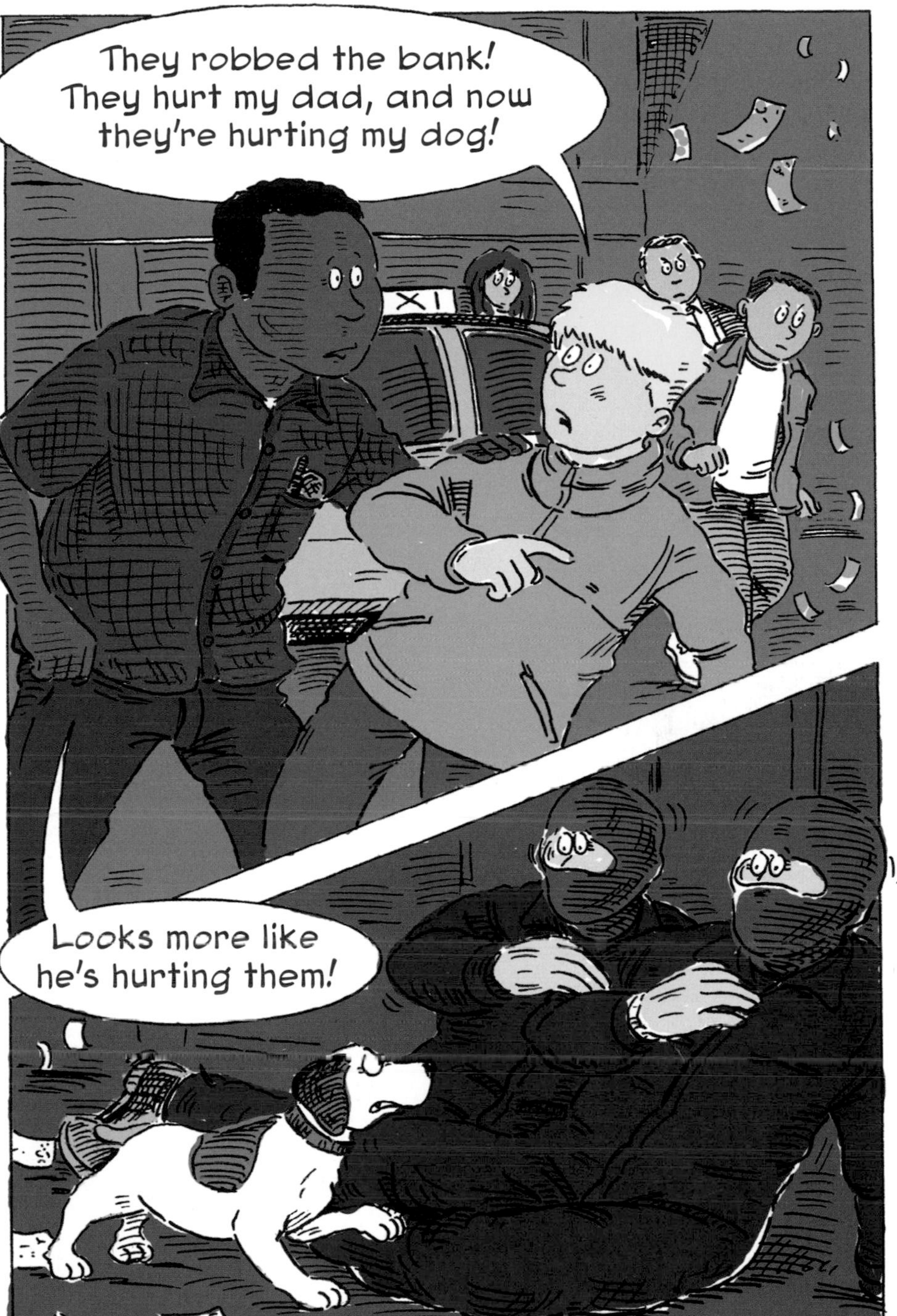
They robbed the bank! They hurt my dad, and now they're hurting my dog!
Looks more like he's hurting them!

The cab driver started to dial 911 on his cell phone as his three passengers ran toward the robbers.

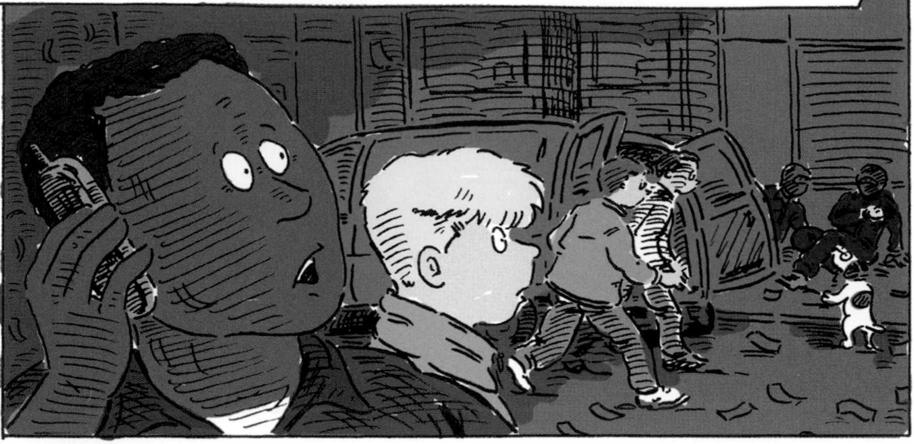

With a squeal of tires, the getaway van zoomed off.

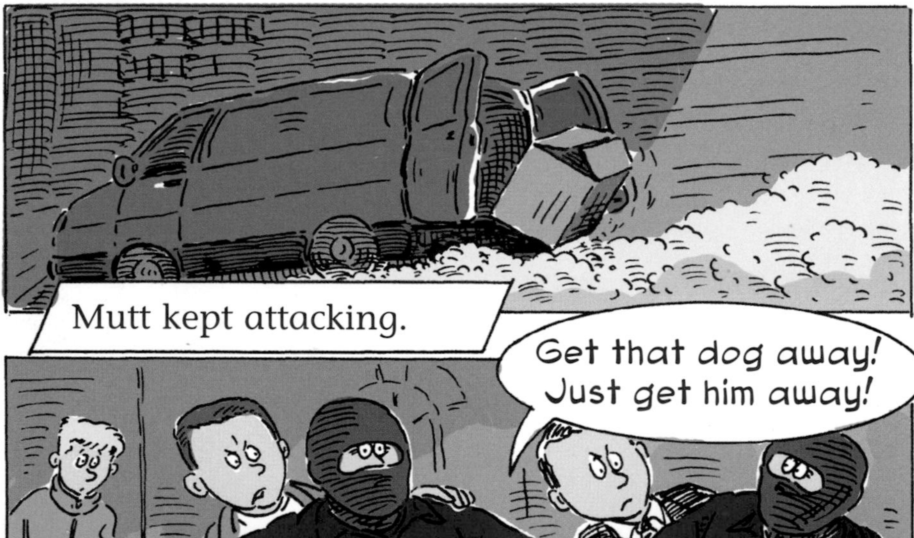

Mutt kept attacking.

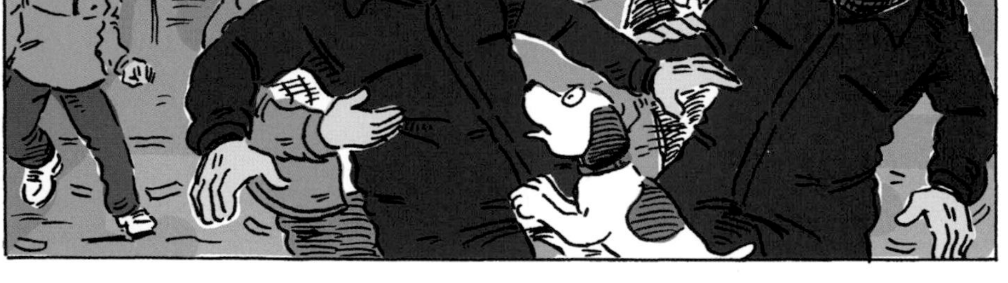
Get that dog away! Just get him away!

CHAPTER SIX

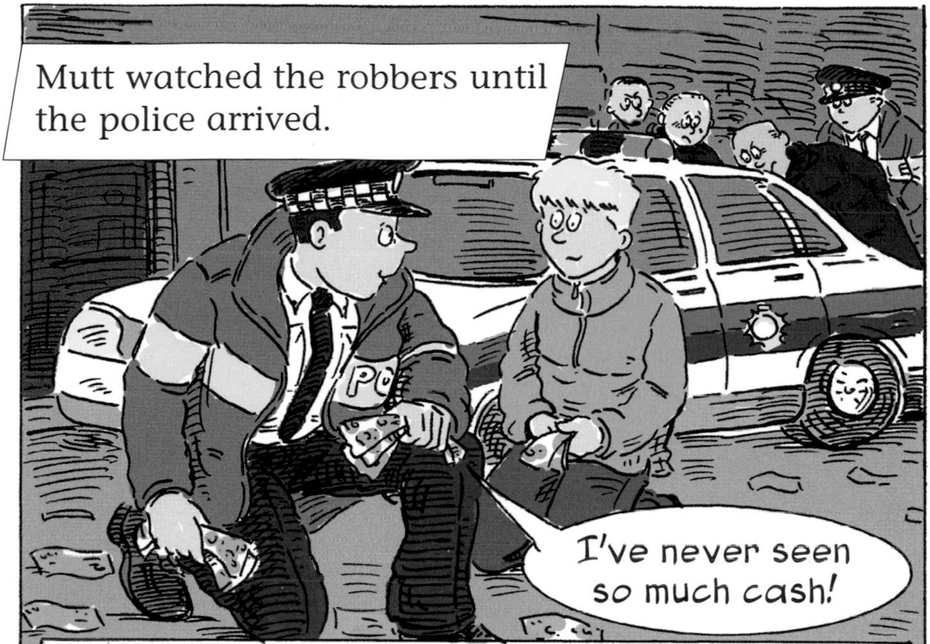

Mutt watched the robbers until the police arrived.
I've never seen so much cash!

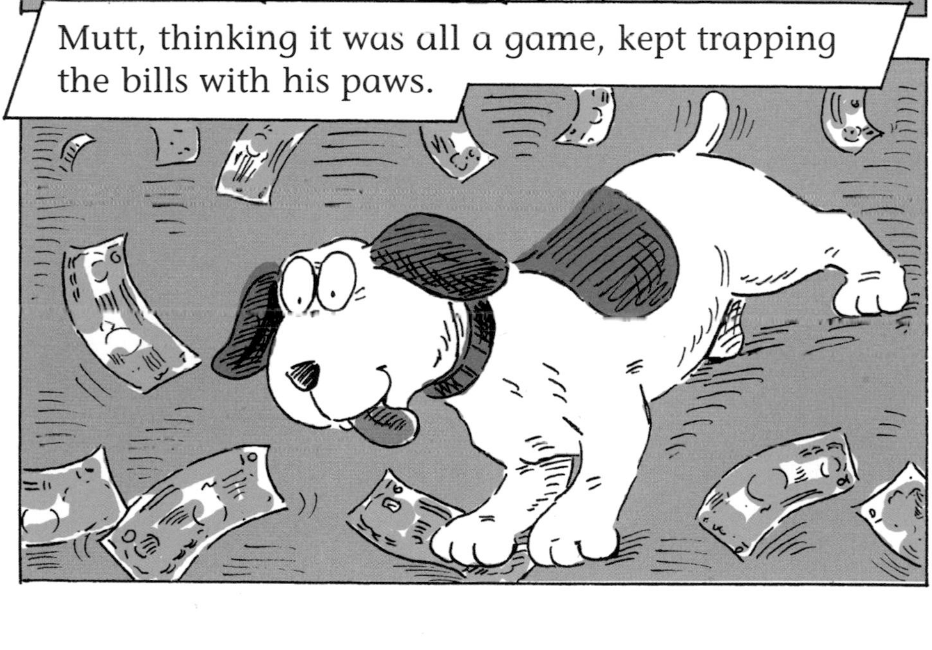

Mutt, thinking it was all a game, kept trapping the bills with his paws.

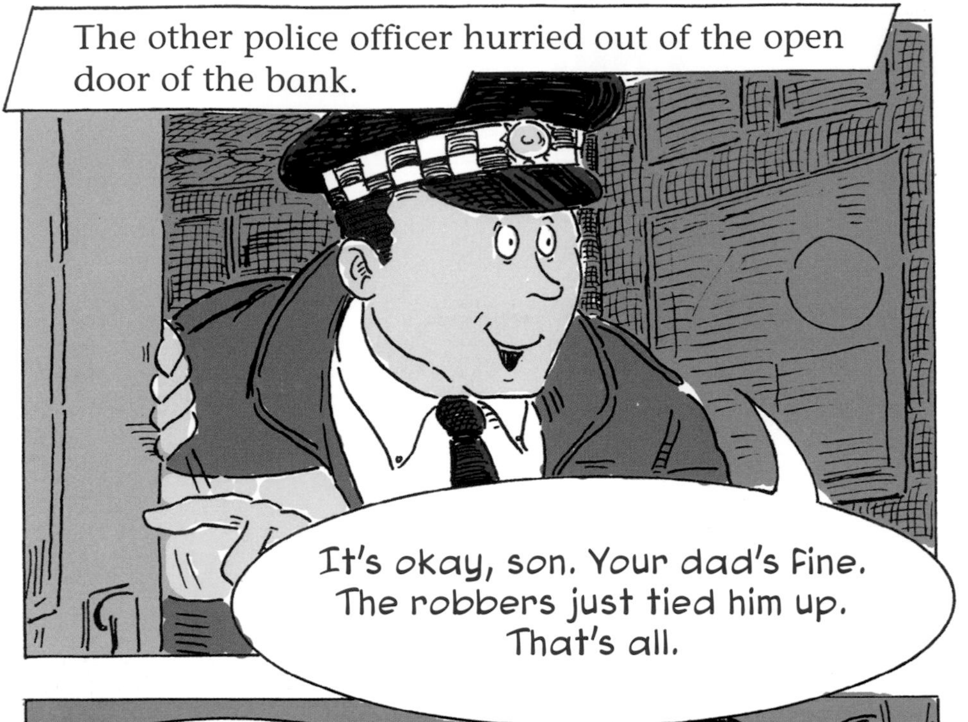
The other police officer hurried out of the open door of the bank.
It's okay, son. Your dad's fine. The robbers just tied him up. That's all.

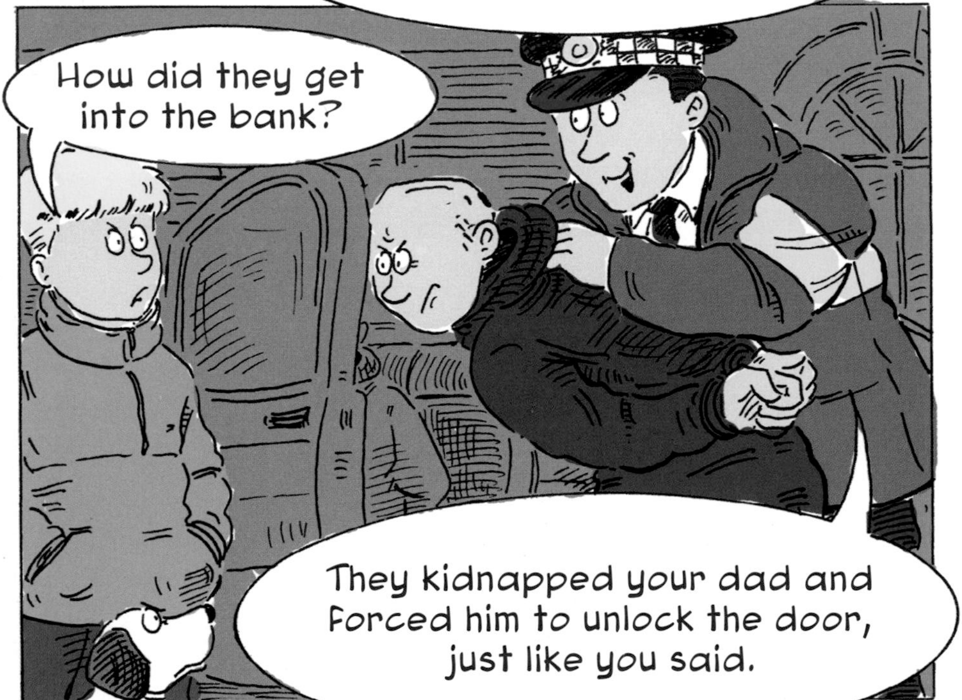
How did they get into the bank?
They kidnapped your dad and forced him to unlock the door, just like you said.

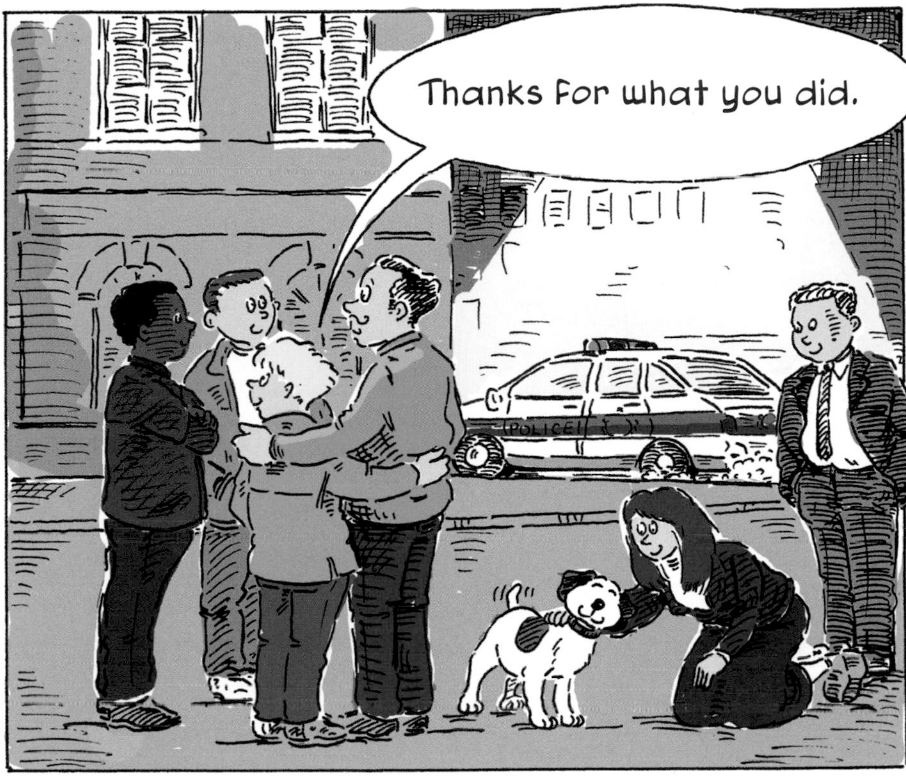
Thanks for what you did.
POLICE

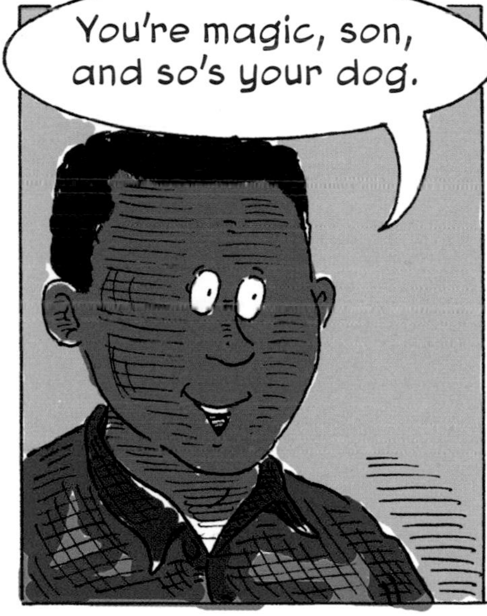
You're magic, son, and so's your dog.

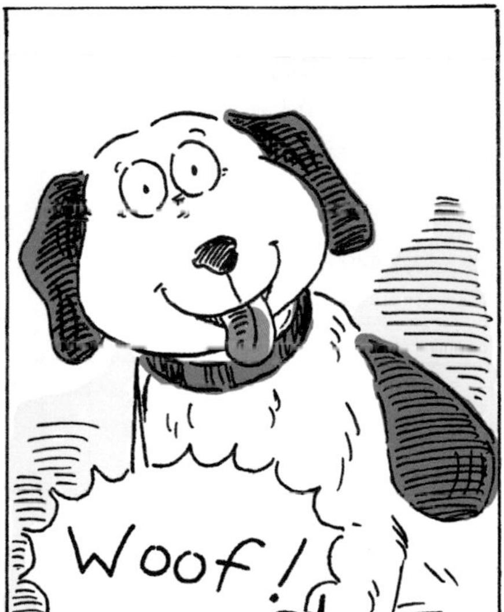
Woof!

CHAPTER SEVEN

Mel and his dad were sitting safely at home after they both made their statements to the police.

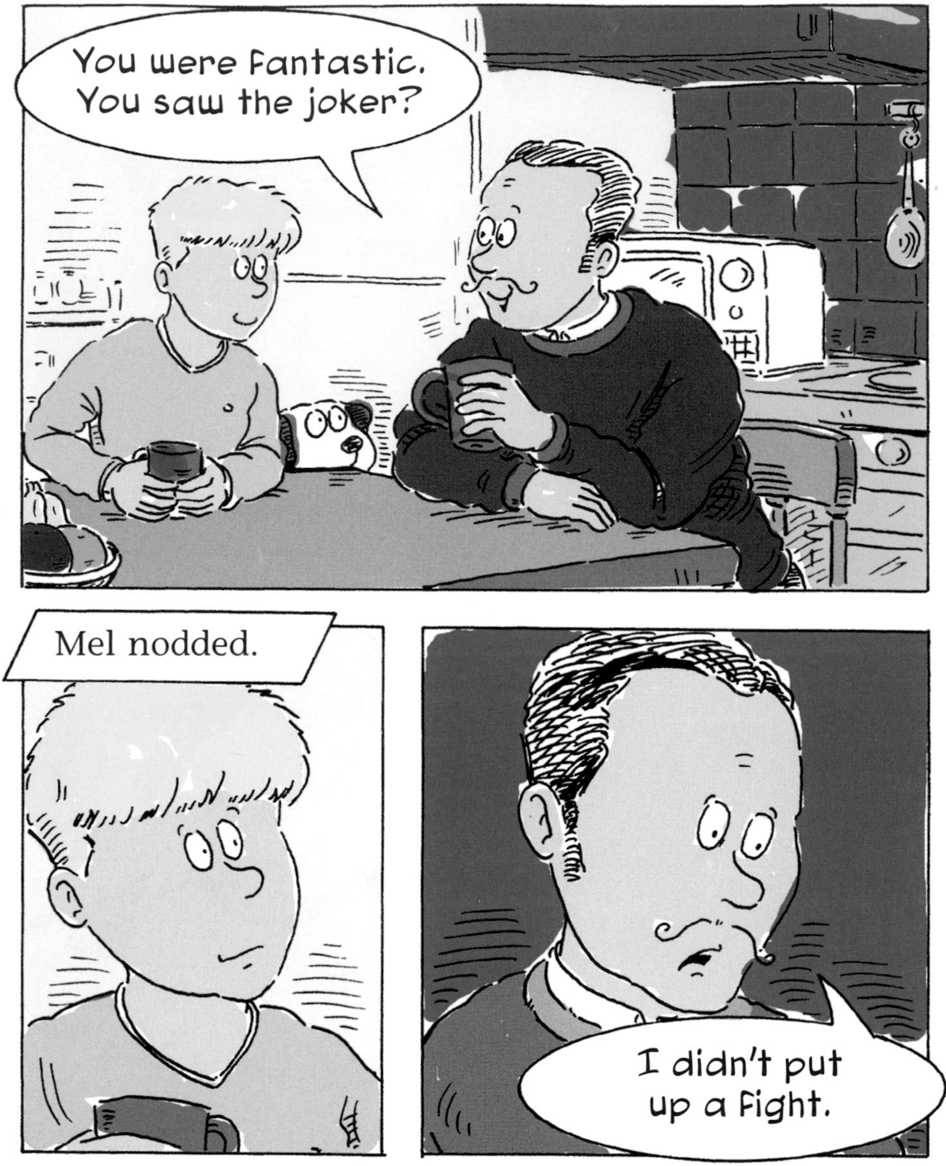
You were fantastic.
You saw the joker?
Mel nodded.
I didn't put up a fight.

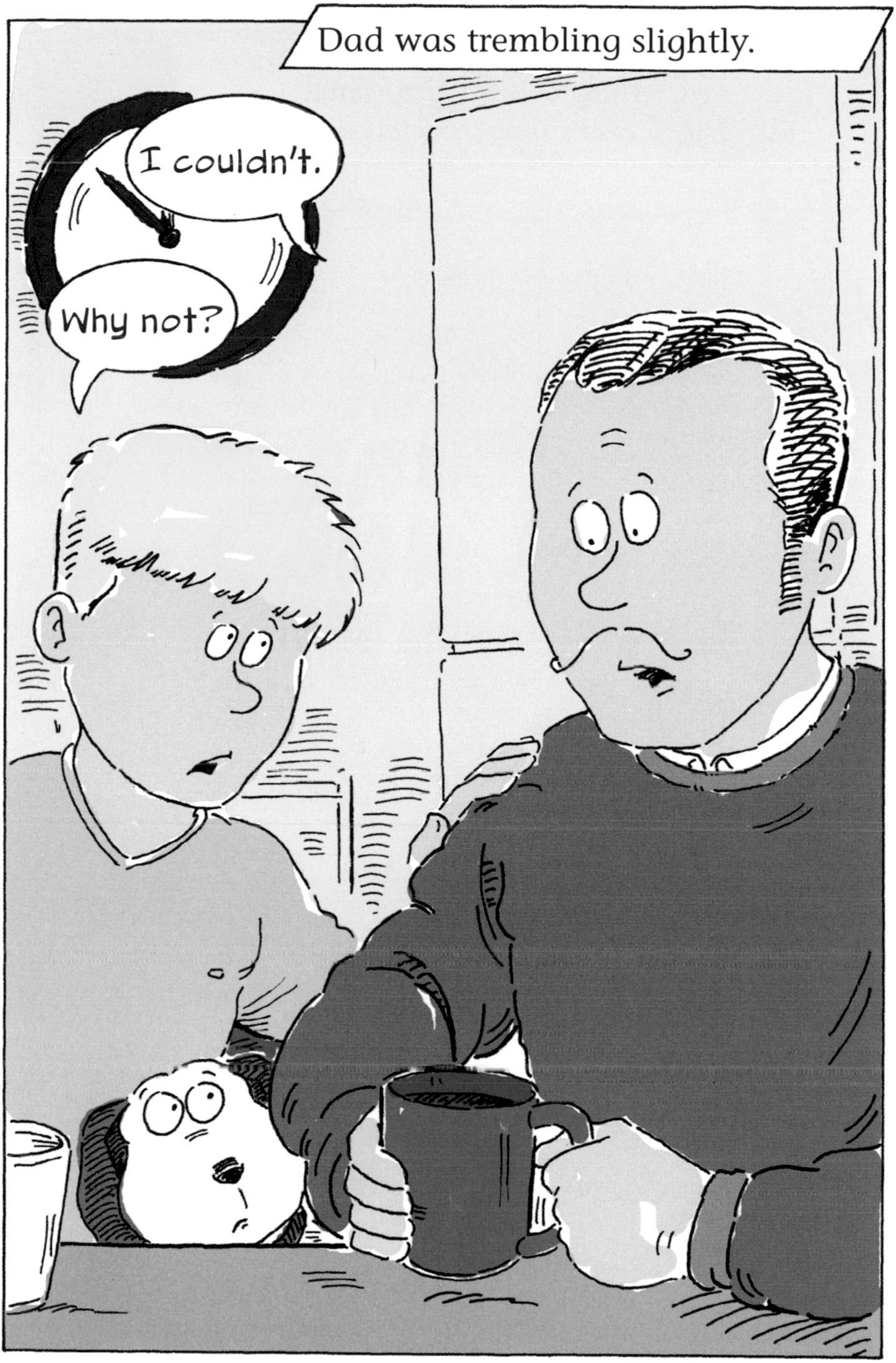
Dad was trembling slightly.
I couldn't.
Why not?

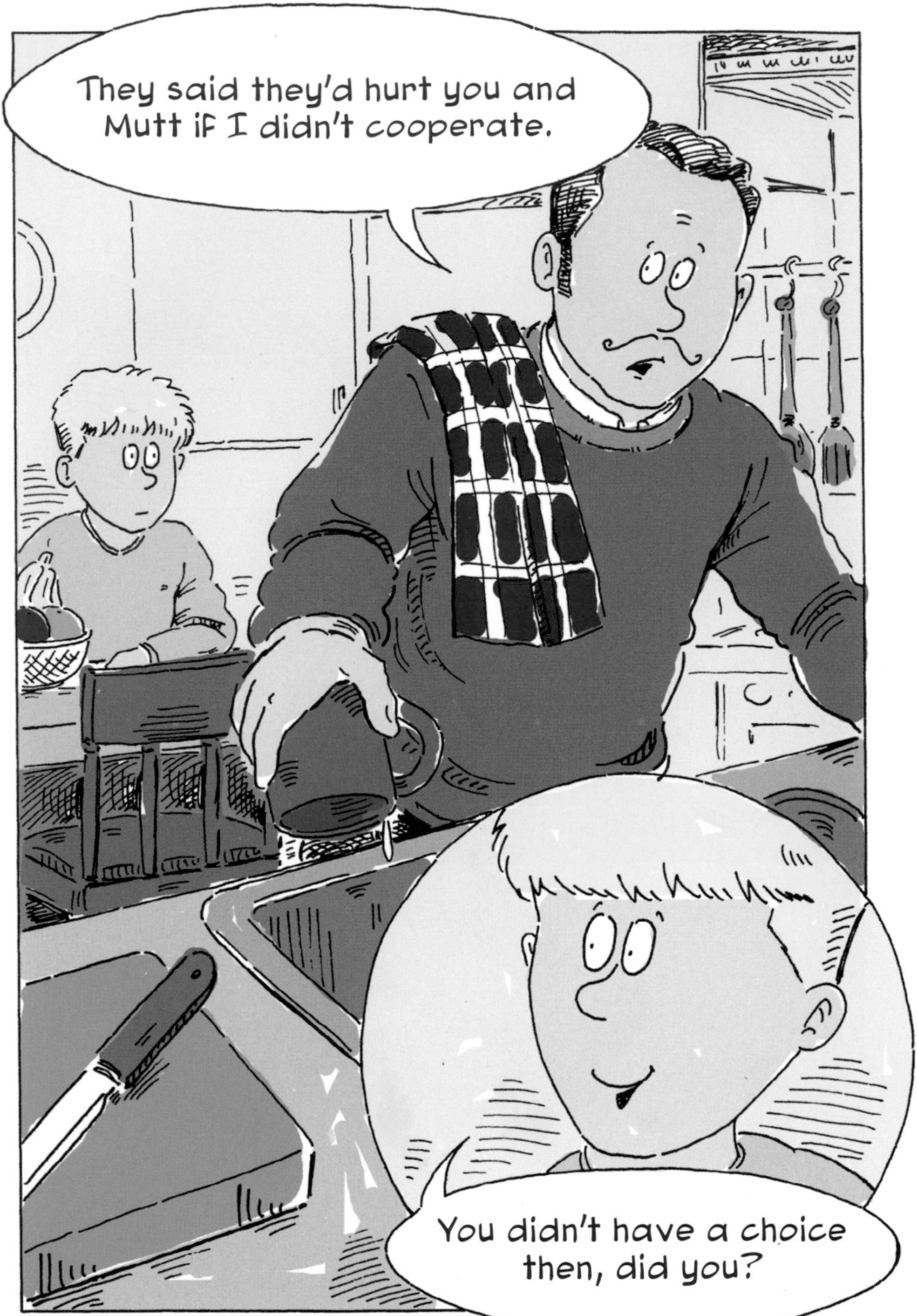
They said they'd hurt you and Mutt if I didn't cooperate.
You didn't have a choice then, did you?

CHAPTER EIGHT

The next week, the town hall was packed. Mel was on stage, and his father was lying in a box on top of a wooden table.

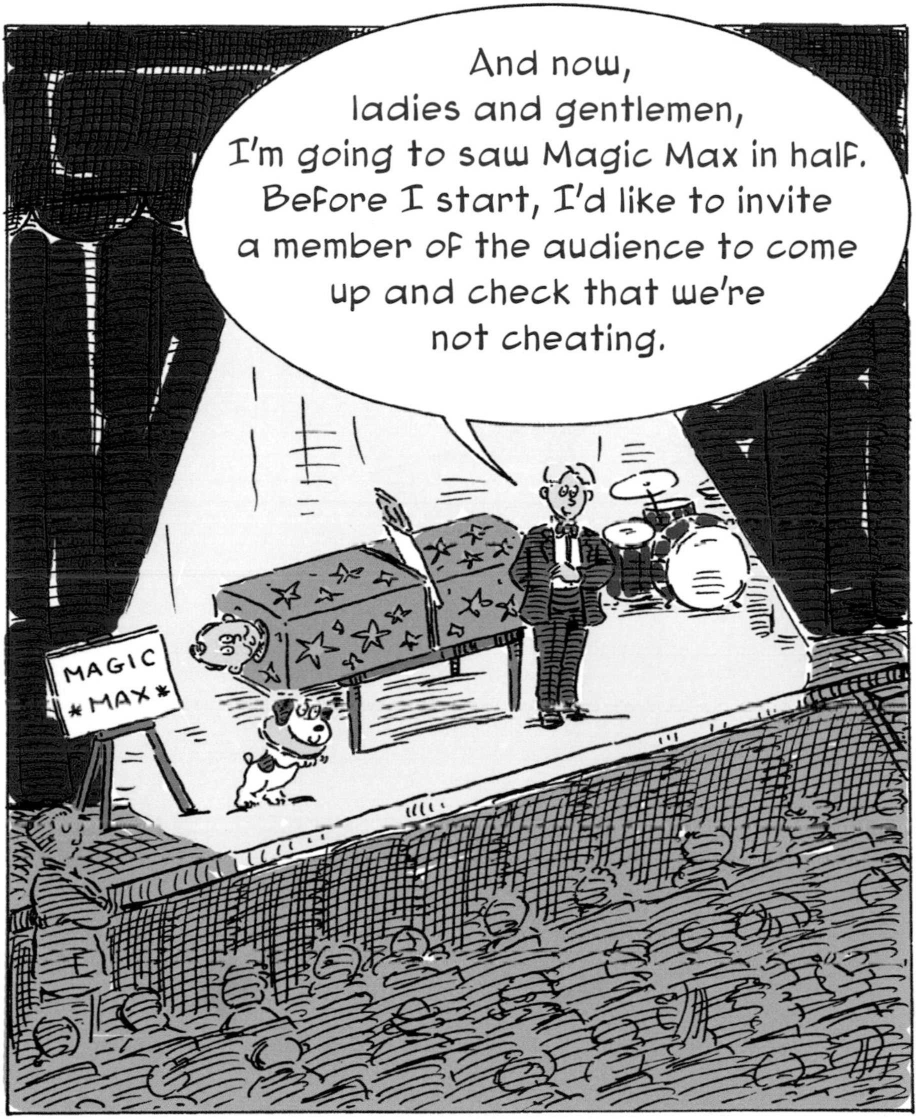

And now, ladies and gentlemen, I'm going to saw Magic Max in half. Before I start, I'd like to invite a member of the audience to come up and check that we're not cheating.
MAGIC *MAX*

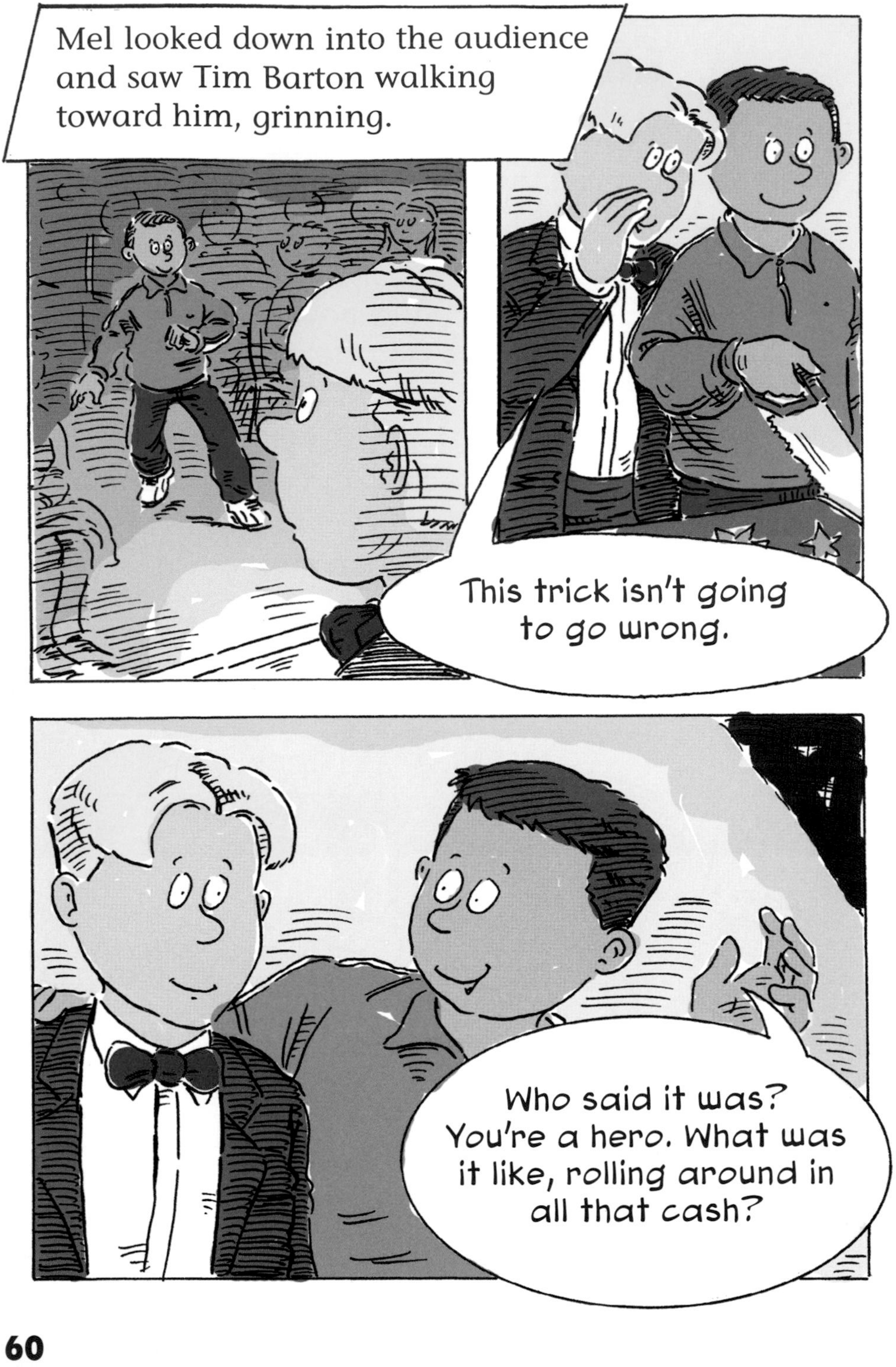
Mel looked down into the audience and saw Tim Barton walking toward him, grinning.
This trick isn't going to go wrong.
Who said it was? You're a hero. What was it like, rolling around in all that cash?

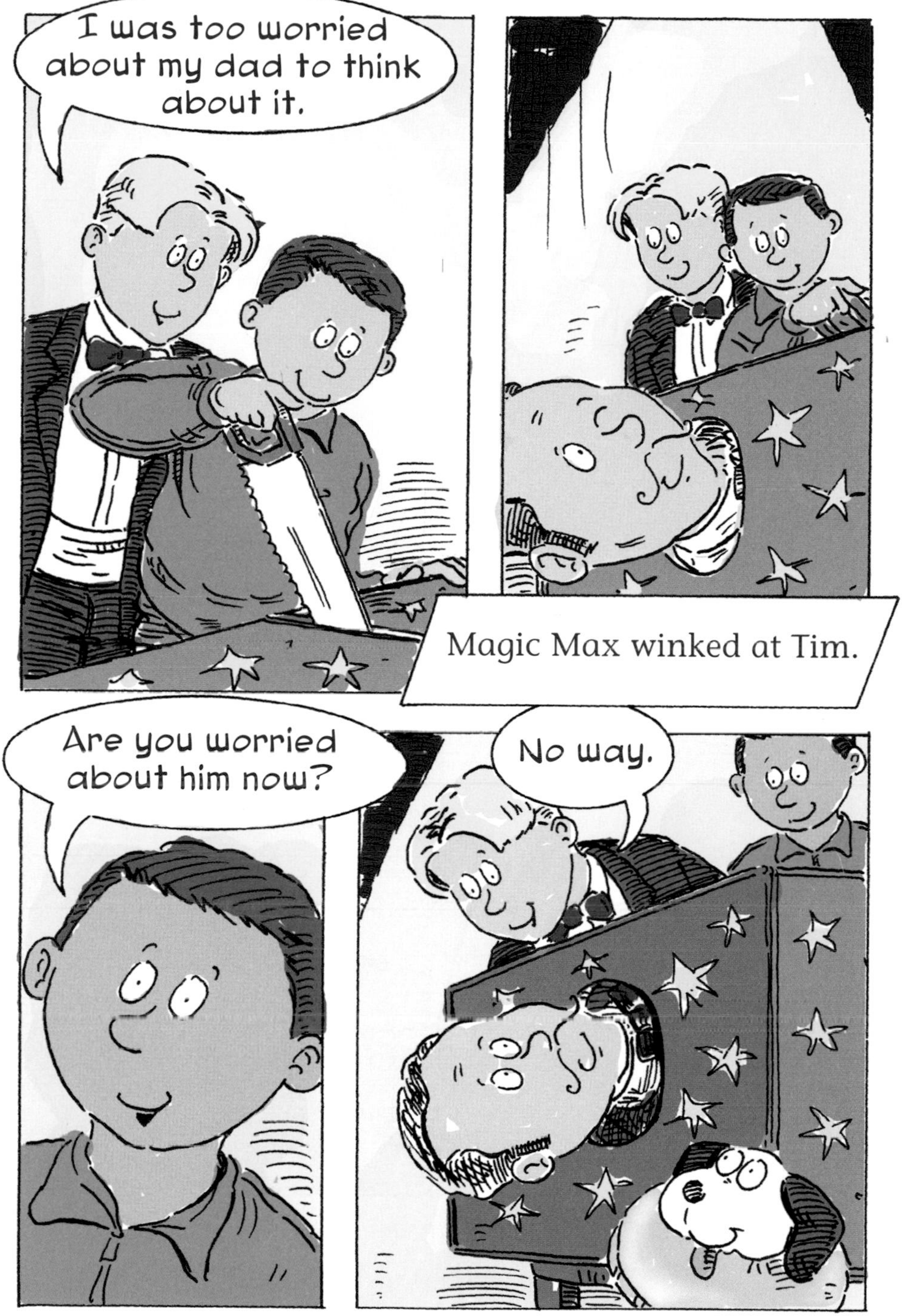
I was too worried about my dad to think about it.
Magic Max winked at Tim.
Are you worried about him now?
No way.

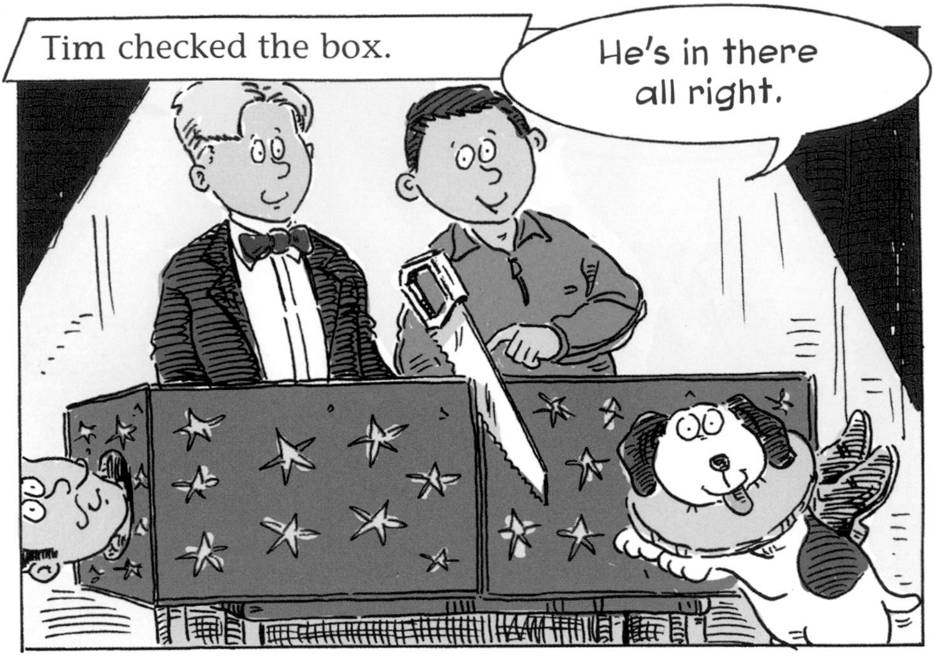
Tim checked the box.
He's in there all right.

Tim looked uneasy as he ran back into the audience, which was tense and anxious.

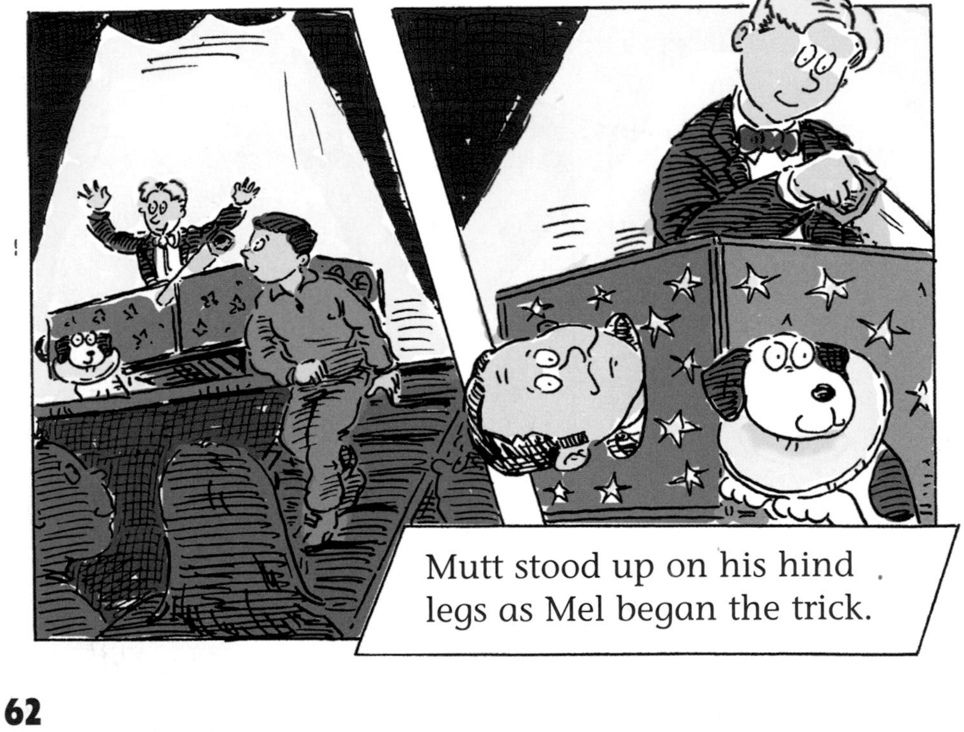
Mutt stood up on his hind legs as Mel began the trick.

Mel's saw made a horrible grinding sound, and some of the audience members screamed as he cut through the box.

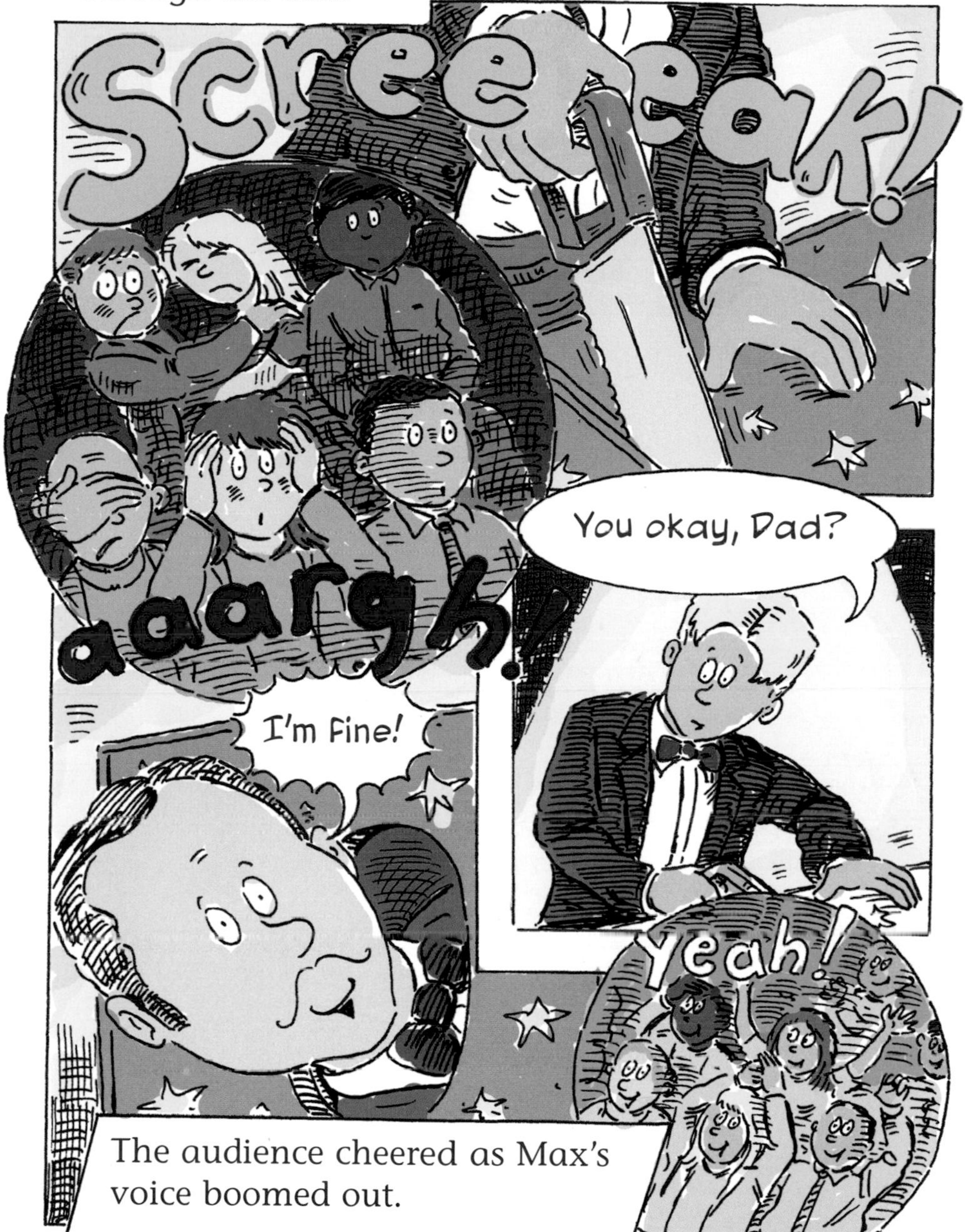
Screeeeak!!
aaargh!!
You okay, Dad?
I'm fine!
Yeah!

The audience cheered as Max's voice boomed out.

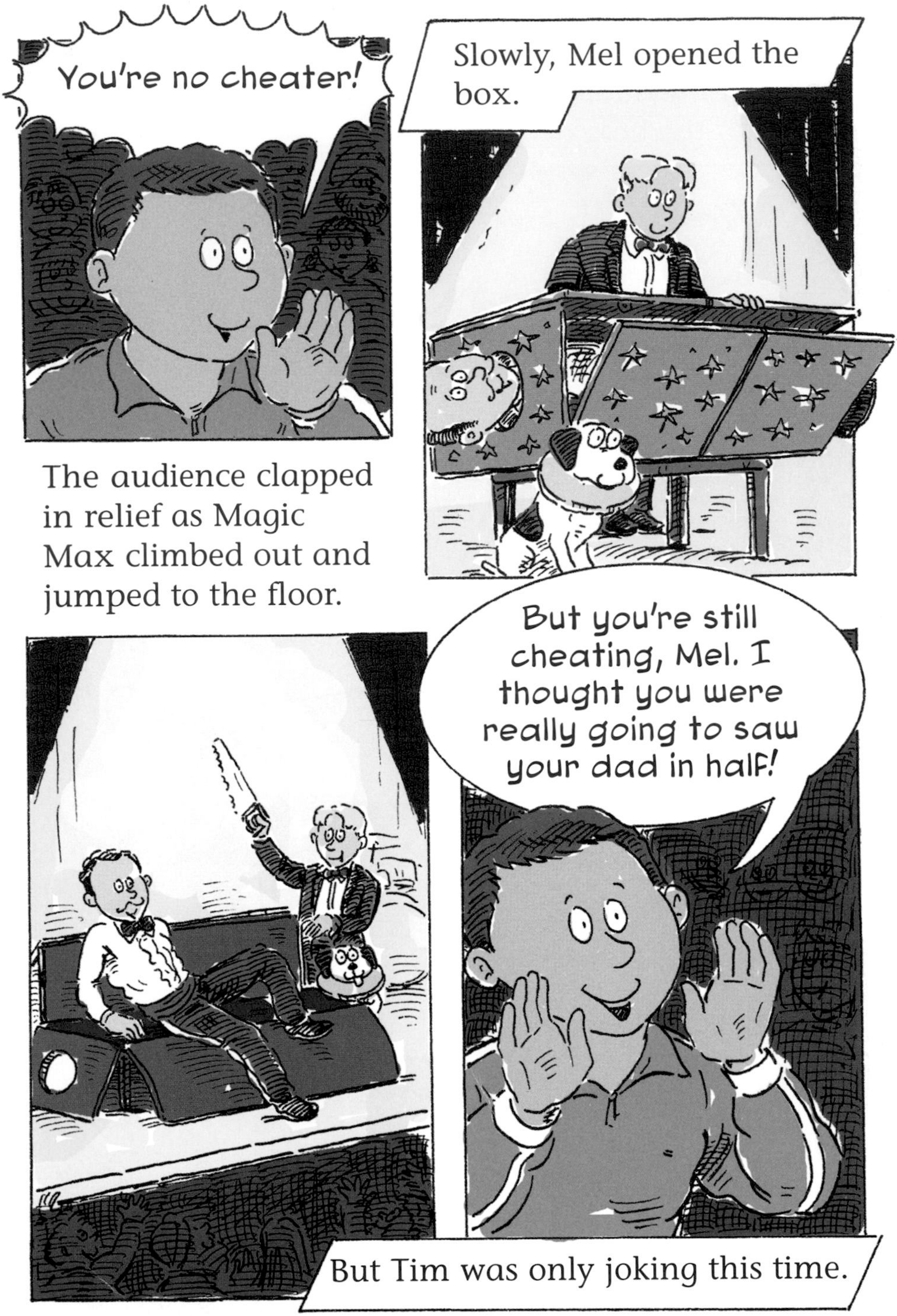

You're no cheater!
Slowly, Mel opened the box.
The audience clapped in relief as Magic Max climbed out and jumped to the floor.
But you're still cheating, Mel. I thought you were really going to saw your dad in half!
But Tim was only joking this time.

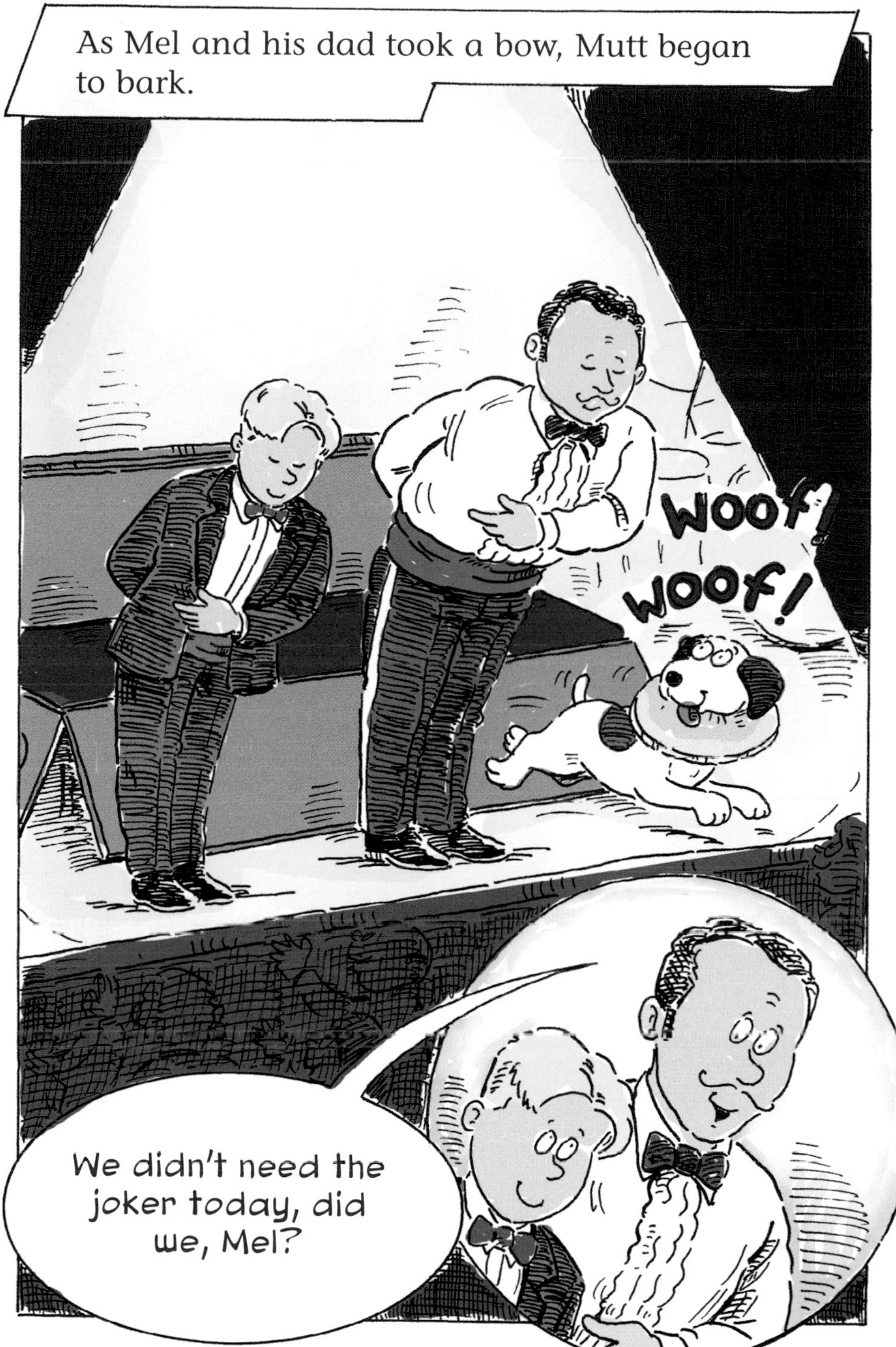
As Mel and his dad took a bow, Mutt began to bark.
WOOF! WOOF!
We didn't need the joker today, did we, Mel?

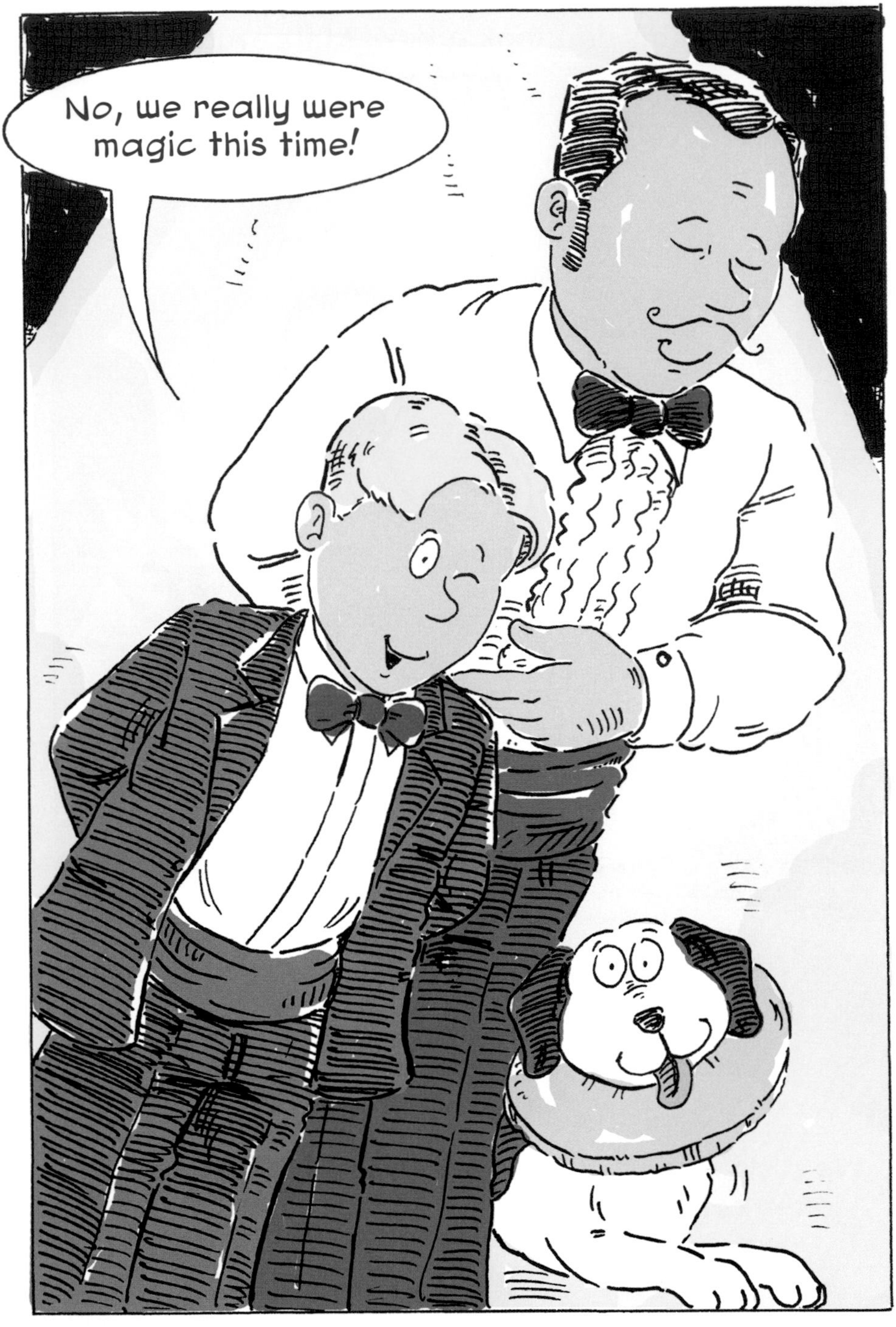
No, we really were magic this time!

ABOUT THE AUTHOR

Anthony Masters wrote many novels, short stories, and nonfiction books for children and young adults. He most recently wrote a children's version of Shakespeare's play *Hamlet* and a young adult series on World War II.

Anthony Masters died in 2003.

GLOSSARY

applaud (uh-PLAWD)—to show that you like something by clapping

audience (AW-dee-unss)—a group of people who watch a performance

concentrate (KON-suhn-trate)—to focus on something

cooperate (koh-OP-uh-rate)—to work together

distress (diss-TRESS)—in need of help

extraordinary (ek-STROR-duh-nare-ee)—very unusual

kidnap (KID-nap)—to take a person from his or her home

magician (muh-JISH-uhn)—a person who does magic tricks

muzzle (MUHZ-uhl)—an animal's nose and mouth

rehearse (ree-HURSS)—to practice before a performance

INTERNET SITES

Do you want to know more about subjects related to this book? Or are you interested in learning about other topics? Then check out FactHound, a fun, easy way to find Internet sites.

Our investigative staff has already sniffed out great sites for you!

Here's how to use FactHound:

1. Visit *www.facthound.com*

2. Select your grade level.

3. To learn more about subjects related to this book, type in the book's ISBN number: **1598890247**.

4. Click the **Fetch It** button.

FactHound will fetch the best Internet sites for you.

DISCUSSION QUESTIONS

1. If you were Mel, would you have tried to catch the robbers by yourself? Or would you have called the police?

2. Tim, the kid who called Mel a cheater, is nice to Mel at the end of the story. What makes Tim change?

3. Mel and his father use the joker card when one of them is in danger. Do you have a signal or sign that you use to tell people when something is wrong?

WRITING PROMPTS

1. Mel and his dad perform together. Have you ever had to perform in front of an audience? Were you nervous? Did the performance go well? Write about what it was like.

2. For Mel and his dad, magic is a hobby that they both enjoy. Write about an activity that you do with a family member or friend.

3. Mel and his dad are stage magicians. Their magic is only make-believe. If you could have a real magical power, what would it be? Write a story telling what happens when you use your power.

ALSO PUBLISHED BY ANTHONY MASTERS

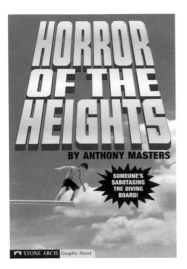

Horror of the Heights
1-59889-030-1

*Dean suffers from a fear of heights —
a big deal if your brother is a diving
champion. Someone is out to sabotage
the diving board that Dean fears. Can
he expose the saboteur?*

STONE ARCH BOOKS,
151 Good Counsel Hill Drive, Mankato, MN 56001
1-800-421-7731
www.stonearchbooks.com